CUSTOMER SERVICE EXCELLENCE

Libraries & Archives

Kent
County
Council

00884\DTP\RN\07.07   LIB 7

THE ELLIE HARDWICK MYSTERIES

THE ELLIE HARDWICK MYSTERIES

Barbara Cleverly

CHIVERS

| British Library Cataloguing in Publication Data available |

This Large Print edition published by AudioGO Ltd, Bath, 2012.

Published by arrangement with the Author.

U.K.   Hardcover   ISBN   978 1 4458 2746 9
U.K.   Softcover   ISBN   978 1 4458 2747 6

Printed and bound in Great Britain by
MPG Books Group Limited

LOVE-LIES BLEEDING

An Architect Ellie Hardwick mystery.

It had taken me two hours to get here. I swished my way, bouncing through the puddles in a haze of falling leaves up the long drive to Felthorpe Hall in north Norfolk. Now, Norfolk isn't Suffolk and that's a fact. The skies are wider, the building flints are bigger, the distances greater, and the cry of the wheeling plover more forlorn. Only fifty miles from home but Felthorpe Hall could never have been in Suffolk.

For the last half hour of my journey through dripping lanes, the rain had eased off, the sun had come out and the whole countryside had taken on a more cheerful cast. But it would still have to work a whole lot harder to please me, I thought resentfully. I drove carefully down the tree-lined carriage road to the Hall, eagerly awaiting my first sight of the ancient house, so praised in the architectural guide I had hastily referred to before I started out. I turned a corner and there it stood by the side of a dark, reed-fringed and heron-haunted lake.

The front door was wide and welcoming, its brick dressings satisfyingly good-hearted and the lowering sun, reflected from its many windows, spoke of ancient warmth. But as I got out of my car I paused and shivered.

'Keep off! Go away!' said the house to me.

'*Deus tute me spectas.*' Said a stone inscription in the parapet. 'Thou, Lord, see'st me.'

All too likely, I thought.

I didn't want to be here. It wasn't my job. I paused for a moment to curse my boss Charles Hastings. The words 'spoilt' and 'manipulative' were as closely associated with his name in my mind as were 'rosy' and 'fingered' with dawn in Homer's. I ought to have seen this coming. Well, the truth was—I had. So why had I gone along with it? For the joy of seeing a house I had never visited before and the satisfaction of arriving by myself and saying, 'Hello, I'm the architect, Eleanor Hardwick.' By myself, not scuttling in Charles's wake carrying the files and the hard hats and answering to the name of 'little Miss . . . er'.

We do a lot of work for the English Country Houses Trust. Of the grandees who run it, Charles appears to have been at school with the few to whom he is not related. And, as our region of East Anglia is thickly strewn with great houses, the practice is a busy one. It was one of the reasons—it was my main reason—for applying for the job of his architectural assistant. Charles calls his Trust work the office 'bread and butter'. I would call it the 'strawberry jam'. I'm mad about ancient

2

buildings. I always have been. And if you're lucky enough to get a job working for an expert in this field and you're based between Cambridge and the North Sea, you've died and gone to heaven!

The lush, rolling countryside seamed with narrow overhung lanes is rich in ancient churches, cathedrals and even a castle or two as well as the old domestic buildings. Down one of the overhung lanes in the middle of the county of Suffolk is Charles' house, a wing of which masquerades as his office. Latin Hall is a fine though eccentric showcase for Charles' skills. For a start, it's thatched, and to go on, it was built in the late thirteen hundreds. Yes, thirteen hundreds. There was still a Roman Emperor on the throne when the foundations were being dug, Charles told me at my interview. A rather debased Emperor perhaps and ruling out of Constantinople but it made a good story for the clients. They were intended to draw the inference—'If this bloke can keep this building standing, he might be able to do something for mine.'

My first autumn working at Latin Hall was miserable. The weather was exceptionally wet and the medieval house leaked badly. The rain-swollen doors stuck, the windows funnelled the icy draughts that knifed down from the Arctic. Charles laughed at my complaints. 'Keep you healthy, Ellie,' he'd said. 'Nothing like a low temperature and a constant air circulation to kill off the bugs! Much better for you to inhale air straight from Siberia than that pre-breathed rubbish they fill your lungs with in London.'

Rain fell in torrents, torrents were followed by gales, tarpaulins blew off roofs and water rose in cellars as it never had before. Every time I looked out of the window thinking that the rain could get no heavier, it redoubled its maniacal and mindless persistence. But there was one source of cheerful amusement for me in all this gloom. Charles had caught a very bad cold. I came in one morning to find him hunched over his desk, clutching a box of tissues.

'For goodness' sake, Charles,' I said, 'go home! You don't have to stay here!' I pointed to the wall chart. 'You've got no meetings today or tomorrow and then it's the weekend. Go home, have a bath, find a good book and go to bed. I'll man the mainbrace,' I finished just to irritate him.

He winced.

'Can't,' he said. 'Just had a call from the Trust. Felthorpe Hall. Main staircase. There's a problem. I've just been looking up my last quinquennial survey report.' He paused and pretended to run a critical eye over it. 'It's rather good, I think. Listen to this, Ellie and mark the style.' He began to read:

'The condition of the main staircase has been mentioned in previous reports and its stability is

4

now a matter of concern. A newel stair with four quarter space landings, its strength is dependent on the support each flight derives from the flight below. Provided tenons are sound . . .' He droned on and I switched off. '*. . . is due to more than shrinkage and old age.'*

'Well, what do you think?'

'I'd say you'd covered yourself pretty well, there Charles. All those provided that's and suspicions of—' I began to say but he interrupted.

'It is always my concern, Ellie, to have a care for the building as well as my own neck. I go on:

'I would suggest that where shrinkage gaps are to be seen, small hardwood wedges be lightly inserted and, if the distortion referred to increases, these wedges will fall. Should this happen, further structural investigation would appear imperative.'

'Don't tell me! Your wedges have fallen?'

'They have. Luckily the house is closed to the public for end-of-season cleaning but they've got some sort of anniversary shindig coming up at Christmas. So they ring me. "Is this staircase safe?" they want to know. What can I say? "Leave it to me. I'll come up and have a look."' He blew his nose dolefully once more, pushed his spectacles up onto his forehead and rubbed his reddened eyes.

His partner was on holiday. There was only one thing I could say. 'Look tell them you can't come until next week or, if there's a panic on, I'll go for you. Why not? I don't think you'll make much sense in your present condition.'

Charles blinked and shivered theatrically for a moment, looked doubtful and then said as though my offer was all so unexpected, 'Well, if you're sure, Ellie, that would be a godsend ... and it's not as though you could do any real damage. I mean, I've laid on a carpenter— Johnny Bell will meet you there at half past two. He's very experienced and ...'

'Just give me the file, Charles! But— Felthorpe Hall? Where is it incidentally?'

'Er . . . North Norfolk,' he had mumbled apologetically.

*   *   *

The house may not have welcomed me but the carpenter, Johnny Bell, greeted me warmly enough in the hallway from which a fine newel stair climbed its way to a dim upper floor. I needn't have come, really. Mr. Bell was perfectly capable of taking up a few boards, dismantling a few stair treads and, indeed, diagnosing the problem and solving it. The architect is very often the third wheel on the bicycle. This was one of those occasions. He knew it and so did I. But with kindly East Anglian courtesy he explained the situation and even managed to make it appear he was hanging on my words.

6

'Didn't like to start until you got here, Miss Hardwick. Thought if we took up a couple of treads here and a floor board on the landing and perhaps the riser off the step up into the pass door, we ought to see what we're up to.'

I was about to say, 'Nails must be cut and punched . . .' but, almost before I could speak, he had slipped a hacksaw under the first stair tread and had started to cut the nails which held it in place. When he'd slipped the stair-treads out of the strings, the risers followed with no more difficulty. We knelt together on the stairs and peered into the cavity which we had created. I held the torch while Johnny Bell felt inside.

'Carriage has gone,' he said. 'It's supposed to be birds-mouthed under the trimmer,' and, feeling along the wall, 'the wall string's gone in the same place.'

I reached into the hole, broke off a section of timber and brought it into the light.

'Death watch beetle,' I said.

'How do you know?' said a voice behind us.

I turned to confront a tall, stooping, bird-like figure peering over our shoulders. He reminded me of one of the bony herons I'd seen on arrival, hunched at the edge of the lake. This was Nicholas Wemyss, the Curator, and introductions followed.

'How do you know?' he asked again.

'If the flight holes are big enough to let you poke a match head into them, it's death watch beetle. If they're only big enough for a pin, it's woodworm—furniture beetle, that is,' I said, as I'd been taught.

'Ah!' said Nicholas, looking impressed. 'Now I really appreciate a complicated technical explanation! But, Ellie, is this serious? Does it mean the stairs are unsafe?'

'Well, it shouldn't be left. Some of this bore dust,' I held out a sample, 'is quite fresh and, no, it probably isn't quite safe.' I looked at Johnny who was nodding in agreement. 'Let's see if we can take up a board on the quarter landing. That'll tell us more.'

Once more the hacksaw blade disappeared under the stair nosing and one by one the ancient nails were snipped through. The first mighty board came loose. Loose for the first time since some ancient carpenter had tapped it into place over three hundred years before. Johnny waggled it to and fro, inserted the end of a nail bar and prised it upwards. 'Can't move it! he said in surprise. 'That's stuck! There's something under there!'

He poked around with the end of a two foot rule. 'Yes, bugger me—there's something under there!'

We watched in puzzlement as he took up a second board. With that obstruction gone the first board came out more easily. But it was unnaturally heavy. It was as much as the two of us could lift and, as it came from its ancient seating, 'Corst blast!' said Johnny 'There's a little old box fastened up to the bottom of that!'

'Little old box, nothing!' said Nicholas. 'No. That's a little old coffin!'

*   *   *

There was no mistaking it. The profile of a coffin lid is in some way branded on the memory. The eternal symbol of death and dissolution, an object of reasonless fear buried in the country memories of us all. It was tiny; not above two feet long. A whiff of profound grief and misery briefly embraced us all as the darkness deepened, the thunderous rain began to fall again and the damp chill of the day sharpened to an icy coldness.

The carpenter ran a knowledgeable hand over the small structure. 'Must have made hundreds of coffins in his time,' I thought.

'Oak boards. Nicely made,' he said, absently caressing the joints with a craggy thumb. 'That were tacked up from below.' He slipped the point of a chisel under the rim of the coffin and pressed upwards against the covering board. 'Lift it off, shall I?'

'No! Wait!' I heard my own voice call out. I didn't want him to take off the lid. I didn't want to see what the box held. 'Perhaps we should call the police? Isn't that what you do when you find a . . . er . . . come across a burial?'

'If that's what it is, it's a very ancient burial,' said Nicholas gently. 'I don't think the police will be interested in something so old. Because it is very old, wouldn't you say?'

'It went in the same day as the staircase was put up,' said Johnny Bell firmly. 'The only way you could get it in with this construction.'

'So we have a date then,' said Nicholas. 'Diana will know. My wife, Diana. She's somewhere about . . .'

'1662. That's the year it was put in.' A low clear voice called down to us from the upper floor. Diana came to join us, taking in the strange scene at a glance. 'Oh, dear! How extraordinary! But how fascinating! Look, with the stairs in their present parlous state I think we should take whatever that is downstairs and put it on the big table in the yellow drawing room and decide what to do about it when we're in no danger of disappearing through a hole. Eleanor is it? Eleanor Hardwick? I'm Diana Wemyss. I was just making you a cup of tea. Perhaps that can wait for a few minutes?'

I smiled as Diana's comforting presence chased away the chill forebodings. She couldn't have been more different from her gaunt husband. Short and rounded with merry brown eyes, she had the cheerful and confident charm of a robin. We all made our way backwards down the stairs and into the drawing room and gathered around the little box waiting for Diana to tell us what to do next.

'We really have to open it,' she said. 'Too embarrassing if we hauled a busy constable all the way out from Norwich to witness us opening an empty container.'

Everyone nodded and Johnny got to work again with his chisel. Hardly breathing, we all peered into the coffin as the lid rose.

'Ah,' said Diana in an unsteady voice. 'Nicholas, perhaps you'd better inform the constabulary? Just to be on the safe side.'

*   *   *

Two hours later, an Inspector had called and viewed the pathetic contents of the box, and had taken brief statements. He agreed that the burial had been clandestine and there'd probably been dirty work at the cross-roads back in the 17th century but, really, this was one for 'Time Team' not the Norfolk Constabulary. He was quite happy to leave it, as he put it, 'in the hands of the experts'. That was us. We were on our own.

On a scatter of almost-fresh sawdust in the bottom of the box lay the yellowed bones of a very small infant. It lay on its side in a foetal position and, as far as our appalled and fleeting glances could determine, there was no obvious cause of death. There was no tattered winding sheet, no identifying bracelet. The only other thing the box contained was a slip of parchment. It had been glued inside the lid and so remained unaffected by the decay within the box. On it a neat hand had written, '*Deus tute eum spectas*'.

'Good heavens!' said Diana. 'What have we here? The lost heir of the Easton family?'

I remember even then in the turmoil of mixed emotions I was feeling that something was off key. I felt sick and guilty that we had, however innocently, displaced and disturbed the little body after all those years. With uncomfortable sideways glances at each other, we had replaced the lid on the coffin, Johnny Bell solemnly making the sign of the cross before packing up his tools and leaving.

Gratefully I accepted Diana's invitation, in view of the late hour and the filthy weather, to stay the night in one of the guest rooms. While she put together a supper in their small flat on the second floor Nicholas invited me to come round the house with him as he 'put it to bed'. I watched him set alarms and lock doors, the whole process taking about half an hour. As we wandered down through the dark house our progress was much delayed by Nicholas's discursions as we passed one beautiful thing after another.

Pausing finally in the gallery which encircled the staircase at first floor level he drew my attention to a run of portraits. 'I'd like to haul this lot in for interrogation, Ellie,' he said. 'I bet one of them could tell us more about the contents of that box. The Easton family. They were all here the year the staircase was put in. They came up from their London home for the jollifications in 1662. The celebrations covered the restoration of the monarchy two years earlier but also the marriage of the younger brother of the Earl.'

He lifted the shade of a table lamp and held it upwards. 'Here he is, with his wife alongside. This is the chap whose anniversary we're celebrating this Christmas. Father of the dynasty. His descendants still live hereabouts—they gave the house to the Trust thirty years ago. Robert Easton took over when his elder brother died childless in 1672.'

I looked up at the handsome florid features of Robert Easton, Earl of Somersham. An impressive man in a curling brown wig to his shoulders, he wore a coat of dark blue velvet with gold frogging over a ruched shirt of finest white linen, a lace jabot at his throat. The painter had conveyed his subject's confidence and pride by the seemingly casual placing of one elegant hand on his hip.

Nicholas for a moment dipped the lamp to illuminate the left hand corner of the painting. I was impressed but not surprised to read: 'P. Lely *pinxit*.'

'A Peter Lely!'

Nicholas smiled. 'Yes, the Dutchman who painted all those sumptuous portraits of Charles Stuart's mistresses. The Windsor beauties. All white bosoms, floating draperies and slanting invitation in their sloe-black eyes. Hmm . . .'

We looked together at the lady in this painting. She was young and fair and quite lovely but here were no sloping shoulders, no flirtatious glance to the artist. Her gown was of chestnut silk, draped and shimmering, and the luscious autumnal colouring was all that you could have hoped for from Lely but worn with an unusual modesty, her only jewellery a simple pearl necklace. In her lap rested a basket overflowing with autumn fruits and flowers—a cornucopia. In the background leaves drifted down from stately parkland trees.

'Mary, Countess of Somersham, as she became on her husband's accession to the title. We assume this was a wedding portrait—it was certainly done in the year of their marriage when Robert was the younger brother-in-waiting. Not much of a catch for a girl, you might think, but he was—for her. She was no aristocrat. Mary was the daughter of a Quaker shipbuilder but very rich so they both got what they wanted from the marriage. An unusual match but it turned out well.'

'And the cornucopia is a pointed reference to the wealth she was bringing to the Easton family?'

'That's right. After the lean years of the Commonwealth it was a miracle they had survived as a family at all and they were certainly pleased to have her injection of cash. Bet if the truth were known she even paid for the staircase! She saved the whole dynasty. She was fruitful in other ways too,' he added, showing me a further picture.

A charming portrait showed seven children gambolling in a landscape which was clearly Felthorpe Hall. Formally dressed miniatures of adults, they played with toys and small spaniels or clustered at the feet of their mother, an older and now matronly Mary. All here was sunshine striking satin, rounded pink cheeks and laughing eyes. An idyllic scene. A perfect family. I said as much to Nicholas.

He grunted. 'Unfortunately, not perfect. There was a fly in the ointment . . . a serpent in paradise. These little poppets had the most appalling uncle. The man destined to inherit the title: William, Robert's older brother. Fortunately for the poppets, the rogue died an early death. A lethal combination of drink and the pox, it's said. He died abroad and spent very little time here at Felthorpe which was held together by the efforts of Robert and his trusty steward.'

The light changed direction again and illuminated a third portrait.

A harsh white face in a black periwig. A diamond ring on a thin white hand lightly holding a small purple flower, a bunch of lace, lidded eyes. A clever face. A voluptuous face. I

15

shivered.

'Wicked William Easton,' said Nicholas.

'Not by Lely, this one,' I said, peering more closely at the portrait. 'But a similar style, surely?'

'It's unsigned and we have no record of the painter. A pupil of Lely? Could be. Skilfully done though. Taken during William's youth, obviously, before he became dissolute.'

I shuddered. 'That man was born dissolute!'

I looked again at the hooded eyes and tried to read their expression. Dark and scornful but there was more—they gleamed with unconcealed invitation. The full lips twisted with a humourless certitude. This man knew he could have anyone he wanted. After more than three centuries he still had the power to make me look away, blushing, repelled and overwhelmed by the force of his flaunting sexuality.

Locking more doors, having first checked that all the rooms were empty, and turning off the last remaining lights, we returned to the landing.

'Hang on! Wait a minute!' I said. 'There's someone downstairs.'

'Can't be,' said Nicholas comfortably. 'There's no one in the house but ourselves.'

'Sorry. For a moment I thought I saw someone under the stairs. Where does that door lead to?'

'Doesn't lead anywhere. It's been blocked

16

for over a hundred years.'

'Perhaps it was the moon?'

'That would be a miracle! No moon through all this cloud.'

We returned quickly to the cheerful, candle-lit dining room under the roof.

*   *   *

It was midnight before, equipped with a spare toothbrush and an old pair of Diana's pyjamas, I was shown to a small spare room on the floor below.

'Hope you'll be all right in here? We'd better aim for eight o'clock breakfast. Suit you? Right then, sleep well!'

It had been a long day and I had hardly been able to keep my eyes open for the last hour but as soon as I reached this little room I knew I was in for a sleepless night. My mind went into unwelcome overdrive. Schemes for the repair of the stairs were uppermost but speculation as to the possible history of the little box and its pathetic contents followed close behind. I got out of bed, drew the curtains and looked out across the park. The moon appeared briefly through a rent in the cloud and a flight of mallard whipped swiftly across this luminous patch.

'And there is nothing left remarkable beneath the visiting moon.'

I wasn't so sure about that!

I climbed back into bed and the unwelcome thought came to me that I needed to make a last dash to the bathroom. I made my reluctant way onto the landing trying to remember where on earth the bathroom was and thankful for the torch that Nicholas had handed me. On my return I was, still more reluctantly, drawn to peer down into the darkness below, prodded by a childish element of self-challenging bravado.

A door opened and shut and a dim figure on the floor below slipped under the stairs and out of sight.

'There is somebody down there! Somebody has got locked in. A cleaner perhaps? But surely the whole place is covered with movement detectors? Who the hell's that?'

My question was answered by a sigh from below and an indistinguishable gabble of words in a female voice. The words ended in a rack of sobbing and I was much afraid.

A shaft of light broke from a suddenly opened door on the floor above and the Wemyss peered down over the balustrade.

'Ellie?'

'Yes?'

'Did you hear that?'

'Yes. There's somebody down there. I thought there was.'

'Can't be,' said Nicholas. 'Can't be.'

They hurried down and joined me. I was very glad of their nearness. The house was

18

desperately cold.

'We heard someone on the stairs,' said Diana.

'That was me going to the loo.'

'No, before that. Did it wake you up?'

'No, I wasn't asleep. But I saw someone just now. And there—look there!'

The tail of a shaft of passing moonlight seemed again to illuminate a dim figure and once again we heard that mutter of pathetic sobbing.

'Come on, Ellie,' said Nicholas. 'Let's go and look at this.'

'You're not leaving me up here by myself,' said Diana.

There was a hiss, a whirr and a metallic click and, after a moment of aged hesitation, an ancient clock struck one.

'If I might make rather a folksy suggestion,' I said, 'would we all like a cup of tea?'

'Now that's what I really appreciate,' said Nicholas. 'The sheeted dead did squeak and gibber in the Roman streets, and the architect calls for a cup of tea!'

*   *   *

'What did Johnny Bell say?' asked Diana when we sat down in the kitchen, fragrant mugs of Earl Grey clutched in shaking hands. 'That the coffin must have been put in when the staircase was constructed? 1660. Then perhaps

Mr. Stillingfleet can help us.'

'Mr. Stillingfleet?' I asked. 'Who's he?'

'Was. Hugo Benedict Stillingfleet. Tutor to the little Easton boys.'

'Wicked Easton?'

'Yes, William and his brother Robert. He was also chaplain and finally steward. He lived here for about fifty years and kept the most wonderful account books—more like a diary really. Every farthing that got spent he recorded it. Everyone who was in the employ of the family and what they earned . . . family journeys, who came to stay and practically what they had for breakfast! If anything funny happened when the staircase was being installed, I bet Stillingfleet has recorded it. Nick, go and get Stillingfleet!'

'I'm not getting Stillingfleet at this time of night! Weighs about a ton and I'm not going down there to unlock the library! It'll keep until morning.'

'That coffin,' I said drowsily. 'That secret little box. Did we release something? Something very small. Something very sad. Did we call back somebody? Somebody who is distressed by the disturbance?'

'We'll ask Stillingfleet in the morning,' said Diana and we finally went to bed.

*   *   *

It was a week before I could return to

20

Felthorpe Hall. Johnny Bell was doing a beautiful job on the stairs and it was nearing completion. The little box still stood safely on the table in the drawing room.

Diana and Nicholas were very subdued. 'We've had terrible nights,' they said. 'The same mutterings and sobbings every night since we disturbed that box! Haven't slept for a week. We don't know what to do. But we've a lot to tell you!'

They led me into the library where the central table was covered in pages of notes and several leather bound and ancient books. With barely suppressed excitement Diana went straight into the result of her researches. 'This is 1661,' she said, one finger on her notes and turning the ponderous pages of the Stillingfleet papers with the other hand. 'Here's the boss telling him to get estimates for "Ye newe westerne stair." And here's Jas. Holbrooke, Master Carpenter, riding out from Norwich to give his estimate—£482.9.2d. Expensive!

'And here we are in 1662. A lot of comings and goings. The family were here for nearly all that year. Lots of company. Ate them out of house and home. Bills for barrels of oysters, anchovies, game birds by the dozen brace, cakes and sweetmeats, sacks of coffee . . . John Fox and his brother Will taken up for pilfering at the Lammas Fair and the good Stillingfleet goes over to the assizes to plead for them.

Successfully, obviously, because they were back on the payroll the next month. And here's one Jayne Marston.'

Diana paused.

'Is she important?'

'Oh, yes, we think so,' said Nicholas.

'Jayne Marston—"Miss Comfort's abigail."'

'Abigail? A lady's maid, you mean?'

'Yes, quite posh. Comes down from London and—note this—without her mistress. And that's odd. This was January. Season still in full swing in the capital. Miss Comfort wouldn't have sent her abigail down to the country for no good reason.'

'Does Stillingfleet give us a clue?'

'Sort of. He refers to her quite often—and affectionately.' She quoted, ' "Ye sorrowful Jayne . . . That forlorn wretch. That sweet slut in her sorrow." Something wrong there, don't you think? And then the staircase gets under way. And in April they start getting ready for a party. Seems to be a belated celebration of the restoration of Charles the Second— the Eastons were all stout monarchists. Economically, they are planning to run it with the celebrations for Robert's engagement to Mary Chandler. Then in June two or three things happen—"Did wait on his Lordship under God's guidance and besought him to remember his creator in the days of his youth, when the evil days come not."'

'That would be William he was beseeching.

And did he remember his creator? Did he do what Stillingfleet wanted?'

'It doesn't say but one rather infers not. And then—dismay and disaster—on the fifteenth of June—"To me at dawn this day comes the swanward early. Jayne Marston, God receive her, found drowned in ye lake."'

Diana turned to me, wide-eyed, 'And she's not in the burial register! She's not buried in the churchyard!'

'Suicide then? Denied a Christian burial.'

'Looks like it. And then William disappears.'

'Disappears?'

'Yes—". . . raging to London", leaving poor old Stillingfleet to unscramble the party. Sounds as though there was the most almighty family row going on.'

'And the staircase?'

'Finished. Here—"Thanks be to God!" Then—and this is where the fun starts—"Twas as though the Devil himself wailed about the house this night and these seven days past. God bless us all."'

'Is that what it's been like for you?'

'Yes. Sobs rather than wails perhaps but going on and on. Just the same for Stillingfleet. At the end of every day he wrote just two words—"No change" until we get to—"All day working in pursuit of my resolve."'

'Working? Working at what, I wonder?'

'Well, in addition to his other

23

accomplishments, Mr. Stillingfleet was a carpenter and turner and he made tables and chairs and he was a bit of a scientist too. He had a workshop. We think it was the little room at the end of the stillroom passage.'

'What do you think he was working at? The coffin?'

'Yes, that's what we think. A secret burial for a tiny child. A child who must have been illegitimate, inconvenient, disposable. Infanticide was sadly common in these days and the rubbish heaps of London, certainly, were where the bodies ended up in large numbers but this child was different. He was special to someone. Someone who was determined to grant him as decent a burial as was possible in adverse circumstances.'

'It's a long shot and we'll never know for certain,' said Diana, 'but listen—Jayne Marston is sent down to the country estate from London without her mistress. Pregnant?'

'If this is her baby and it was born in June,' I said hurriedly calculating, 'she would have been three months gone in January and just beginning to show . . . yes, the right moment to send her into obscurity. But is this consistent? Is that what the family would have done? Wouldn't they have just turned her out of the house?'

'I don't think so—not then. This wasn't the Protectorate, this was the Restoration. Cavalier politics and Cavalier morality.

Cavalier kindness if you like. And all the evidence from Stillingfleet is that the Eastons treated their servants with consideration. He was himself almost part of the family. They couldn't have functioned without him. But suppose I'm right. Suppose Jayne comes down to Norfolk because she's pregnant. Suppose Wicked William is the father. Suppose he comes down for the party and takes no notice of her or spurns her and perhaps that was what Stillingfleet was begging him to remember, begging him to do something for the wretched girl. Then the baby is born and is still-born? Or dies perhaps?'

'Dies? How? And where?'

'We'll never know,' said Diana slowly. 'Let's just say the baby dies. The body must have been hidden away. There is no recorded death of an infant at that time. Perhaps Jayne at the death of her child goes demented and throws herself into the lake?'

'Did she fall or was she pushed?'

'I'm sure Stillingfleet knew but he's not saying. Loyalty to the family. It was only a servant involved, I know, but this was an isolated community where a scandal would have torn through the county and don't forget that most people up here were still rigidly puritan in their outlook. William would have had a bad time of it if it had come out.'

'At any rate, there was no Christian burial for Jayne's child, no baptism even

25

and this would have been a horrifying thing for the mother. The child would have been condemned to eternal perdition.'

'And this is when the nightly wailing starts?'

'Yes. But Stillingfleet knows what to do. He makes a little coffin. He places the body inside with a copy of the words from the family motto.'

'Wait a minute though—It's not quite the right wording, is it? Look at the third word. The motto is, *"Deus tute me spectas"*. It should say "me". "Thou God see'st me" but this says "eum". "Him". God sees him. Who?'

'I thought it might mean—"God watch over him"—the child, that is.'

'No. *"Spectas."* It doesn't mean look out for in the sense of watching over, it means—see, look at.'

'Well, I think this is as close as he dares get to an identification, a direct link with the Eastons. And one night, as the staircase is nearly finished, he fixes it up under a floorboard, replaces the floorboard and says a burial service over it. It was the best he could do.'

'Any more from the diary?'

'Only this, but significantly—"Under the hand of God, I pray, I finish my work and, all praise to Him, a quiet night at last."'

We sat for a moment in silence. 'I bet that was it, or something very like that,' I said. 'All quiet until I came along with a nail bar. What do we do now?'

'I've been thinking about this,' said Diana. 'Look, Johnny is still here working on the stairs. Do you think we could just put it back again? Say a few words perhaps?'

'Yes, I'm sure we could do that,' I said.

We laid it back in its place and Johnny tapped nails back into position through the rim the thoughtful Hugo Stillingfleet had left for this purpose. The new nails sank in easily. We stood back and looked at each other uncertainly.

'May he rest in peace and light perpetual shine upon him,' said Diana quietly and clearly.

*   *   *

But something was worrying me. We had worked out a solution of sorts to an intriguing puzzle but I hadn't heard that satisfying click as the last piece of the jigsaw falls into place. We had heard the truth, I was sure, from Stillingfleet but had we heard the whole truth? I didn't think so.

I went to look again at the Easton portraits. I remembered Nicholas had said he would like to interrogate them. Well, why not? I thought I knew the right questions to ask and I thought Peter Lely and his unknown pupil had given their subjects a voice which could still be heard over the years. I had released something which had lain dormant but only just contained through the years and now I believed it was calling out for resolution and justice. The Norfolk Police weren't interested in knowing who had committed infanticide and possibly a second murder all those years ago but I was.

I managed to evade the hypnotic stare of Wicked William and concentrated first on the sunny opulence of the wedding portrait. Robert and Mary. Even the names were reassuringly solid. Following the painter's clues, I knew that this couple had married in the autumn, their betrothal according to Stillingfleet had been in the summer of 1662 and presumably Robert had been pursuing this heiress during the previous London season. At the very time Jayne Marston had been sent away to the country. Had he known the sorry story of his sister Comfort's maid? It was a family with a reputation for large-heartedness in its dealings with its retainers. Yes, he would have known. He would have been concerned. But concerned perhaps for another reason.

Mary's fortune had saved the family and guaranteed his position in society. Robert would not have welcomed any breath of scandal to do with the family his golden goose was about to marry into. 'Of Quaker stock' Nicholas had said. I looked again at the heart-shaped face, framed by wispy golden tendrils, the modest dress, the tightly pursed lips and I wondered about Mary.

'Was it to avoid offending *you*?' I murmured, 'that Jayne and her child were done away with? Too inconvenient, too vocal, a servant, yes, but so intertwined with the family she had forgotten her place and was making herself a nuisance? Would it have ruined Robert's schemes if you'd discovered that his brother had seduced a family maid?'

I couldn't believe that.

'And why did you flee?' I asked turning at last to William. 'Why didn't you just tough it out?' An Earldom, the King's supporters back in power again—the future looked good for William Easton. What was he really fleeing? Not a family scandal—there must have been something more.

The dark eyes taunted, enticed, seduced. I speculated again about the identity of the unknown painter and was struck by a devastating thought. A thought so obvious and yet so shocking I groped my way to a Chippendale chair and, against all the house rules, sat down on it. The painter's message now screamed out at me. How could I not have seen it before?

I heard Nicholas leaving the library and called out to him.

'Ellie? You ok?' He hurried to join me.

'We've got it all wrong, Nicholas!' I said. 'Come and have a look again at Wicked William. He's been wrongly accused! It couldn't have been him!'

I positioned Nicholas in front of the portrait. 'Now, imagine you're the painter. And that, of course, in the 1660s, means you're a *man*. The sitter is reacting to you. What do you see?'

'Oh, my God!' said Nicholas. 'I see it! And to think that all these years women have been blushing and averting their eyes thinking he was trying to seduce them. He wasn't at all, was he?'

'No. He was flirting with the young apprentice who was painting him. And, judging by the resulting image, the interest was reciprocated. I'm not sure they had a word for it in Cavalier England but this chap was gay and proud of it, you'd say.'

'I'm certain they didn't have a word for it in north Norfolk! And it was a capital offence at the time. "Death without mercy" according to the Articles passed by parliament in 1661. He could, technically have been executed if discovered.'

'What if he were discovered?' I speculated. 'Caught in flagrante with a handsome young painter, let's say?'

'He'd have had to flee to somewhere more worldly—to France . . . to Italy . . . Poor old Stillingfleet, holding all this together! But this is just guess-work, Ellie.'

'Oh, yes. But look at his hand, Nick! Do you see the flower he's holding?'

Nicholas peered at the tiny purple face.

'Always assumed it was a violet but it's not, you know! It's Heartsease. Common little English flower. It's got lots of names—Love-Lies-Bleeding, Love-In-Idleness, la Pensée in French, wild Pansy.'

'Exactly! Pansy! A badge. The seventeenth century equivalent of a pink ribbon. That's what you'd call flaunting it! So how likely is it that he'd be spending time in London undoing a lady's maid? Possible, I suppose—but I can't see it! No. I think we've got to look elsewhere for the father of that little scrap in the coffin.'

Our eyes turned on Robert's handsome countenance. I waved a hand at his line of progeny. 'It's pretty obvious in which direction his preferences lay!' I said with more than a touch of bitterness. 'And he had such a lot to lose if his puritan bride-to-be were to catch him with his hand up a maid's skirt! Mary doesn't look the understanding kind to me!'

I looked at the pair in disgust. Their faces had taken on a cast of smug respectability. Their innocent children, healthy and happy, had thrived perhaps at the expense of that other unwanted child.

Suddenly I found myself playing the role of judge in this case that would never come to court and I knew what was required of me. I knew the formula that would ensure undisturbed nights for Diana and Nicholas.

I spoke aloud to the portrait and to anyone else who was listening on the stairs. 'Robert

Easton, I find you guilty of infanticide,' I said simply. 'May God have mercy on your soul.'

'*Deus tute eum spectas,*' said Diana who had come silently to join us. 'God is watching him. God knows what he has done.'

* * *

A week later Charles waved a postcard at me.

'Not much in the post. It's for you from some boyfriend of yours in Norfolk. A picture of a bloke in a periwig and it says, "Thank God! At last a quiet night! Eternally grateful, love Nicholas." What *did* you get up to in Norfolk, Ellie?'

HERE LIES

An Ellie Hardwick, Architect, Mystery.

The two bodies were lying side by side in the south aisle of the church of Tilbrook St. George.

The figure on the right, an armoured knight, his hands folded in prayer, his feet resting on a lion, was impressive enough but it was the pallid alabaster beauty of the lady at his side which seized and held my attention. Her delicate hands were peacefully folded below her breast, her feet rested on a tasselled cushion. The knight had lain here in this quiet place carved in white stone for nearly six hundred years. His lady was of flesh and blood and was newly dead.

He had a dagger at his side; she had a dagger in her heart.

I might have run screaming from the church. I ought to have checked for a pulse. I did neither of these practical things. I stood and stared. And it occurred to me even then that I was reacting to the scene as I was intended to react, for, in that moment of terrified discovery, the macabre display was not only weirdly beautiful but full of meaning.

The early morning sun angled through the stained glass windows, stencilling the pammet floor with a pattern of rich colour: vert, gules and azure. The heraldic colours sprang easily to mind in this medieval setting. The peaceful couple were framed by a canopy of sunlit stone. Sir John Hartest, survivor of the Battle of Agincourt, lay in plate armour, gauntleted hands resting on his chest, helmeted head encircled by a jewelled wreath. At his left hip, on a richly sculpted baldrick, was carved a dagger with an ornate gilded hilt. His features were serene; as the sunshine slid across his face he seemed almost to smile.

At first sight his lady appeared no less serene. Closed eyes, a dreaming face, her pallor a match for his alabaster. Her long fair hair had been arranged to frame her face before spilling over the edge of the tomb, the long white dress she was wearing had been carefully draped and folded. I brought my eyes back to her breast and to the head of the dagger, very slightly to the left and very precisely into the heart.

I started as frozen emotion began to break up and run again and the paralysing spell of the scene lost its grip. I looked away and then forced myself to focus once more on the dagger. But how could it . . .? Surely not! I peered more closely at the hilt, professional curiosity taking over for a moment. And then I looked back at the one at Sir John Hartest's side. A representation of a vicious stabbing dagger possibly of Spanish manufacture and designed to penetrate plate armour with a short, underhand stroke. A misericorde. The word meant compassion—pity. Such blades were often used to put dying soldiers out of their misery on the battle field. What kind of sick trickery was I witnessing?

The carved stone dagger and the wrought steel dagger were identical.

I had the clear impression my presence had been conjured up to bear witness to this theatrical offering. My fingers, of their own accord it seemed, reached for the camera I always kept slung around my neck when I'm working. Slowly I raised it and framed the scene. The shutter clicked and a zillion pixels preserved the horror on the memory card of a Nikon slr.

With trembling fingers, I took out the memory card and replaced it with a spare. Wondering at my motives and with, already, a vague concern for police searches and confiscations, I tucked the original one into an inside pocket

The click was discreet but enough in that deep silence to shatter the Sleeping Beauty bewitchment of the tableau. It was fading rapidly now and reality was crowding in. Hasty and fearful, I looked round the church, belatedly considering the possibility of a murderer lurking, watching me react to his work. Behind the pews? Under the velvet hangings? In the vestry? There were hundreds of places to hide in a medieval church and I knew them all. My eye roamed over the nave and was caught by the grotesque and inquisitive features of a carved oak devil, one of the bench end figures, eager, apparently, to enjoy this violent event which had shattered his centuries of unwelcome peace. Imperceptibly, the sun changed its angle and a rosy glow began to creep over the white cheeks of the dead girl, infusing her with life.

Not with a shriek, but with a very female whimper, I fled down the aisle, terror snapping at my ankles, towards the heavy oak door. In my panic I wrestled with the massive box lock and the more I pushed, the more firmly the door remained shut. Was someone standing outside laughing at me? Or, and the thought made me whimper out loud again, was someone standing *inside* laughing at me? With a dry rustle and a clearing of the throat, the ancient machinery of the church clock gathered itself and launched into its ten o'clock strike. The chimes rang out over my head deafening and confusing me. A malevolent woodwose in the spandril of the doorway sneered down at my pathetic attempts to get out.

'Stupid cow!' I gained a little control by swearing at myself.

I gained a little more by remembering that I should be pulling the door, not pushing and a second later I had worked the trick of holding down the latch and tugging the door at the same time.

I erupted into the blessed spring sunshine, the cheerful birdsong, the cool breeze of a Suffolk morning.

*   *   *

I'm an architect. I spend my life working in old churches and ancient buildings—that sort of architect. I've seen ghosts—it goes with the job. I've unwittingly addressed a few words to one or two, I've even held a perfectly sane conversation with one, but I had never been truly terrified in an old building before. I ran down the path towards the safety of my old Golf.

In the deep shadow of the lych gate I cannoned off a hard body marching briskly in the other direction.

'Hey! Watch it! Where are you rushing off to?' came a startled male voice. I looked up to see what must be my client, the man with whom I had a ten o'clock appointment. My client, Edward Hartest, or, as his letter head had it—The Honorable Edward Hartest J.P.

'Not fleeing the field already are you? For God's sake, Miss . . . er . . . the clock's only just struck! I take it you *are* my church architect?' He tapped the top of my hard hat. 'Well, of course. Who else would wear one of these ugly things? Hang on—you're upset! Has

something happened? Now look here, Miss
. . . er . . . I don't know what's happened but
hysterics won't help. Pull yourself together if
you can and tell me what's going on here!'

He smelled of hay and diesel oil. Not
unpleasant and the slight whiff of *Givenchy
Gentleman* was reassuring. My grandfather
used it. He was wearing an ancient checked
shirt and jeans, the uniform of a farmer in
May. I didn't like him much and I certainly
wasn't going to be patronised by him. I glared.

'Can' t talk to you now! I've got to get to my
mobile! I left it in my car.'

He stood aside waving me past him with
mocking formality and watched me, quizzically
enquiring while I fumbled to unlock my Golf.

'Mobile indeed!' he scoffed. 'You young
people are so dependent! Just how many
friends do you have to inform that you're at
the church?' He looked pointedly at his watch.
'Busy man, you know. No time to stand about
listening to a string of inanities and whatever
else does one hear spoken on those things?'
He curled his lip at the sight of my cell phone
emerging from the glove locker.

Praying that my battery would not be flat, I
stabbed out 999.

'Hello? I want the police please.'

Pause.

'Police? There's a dead body in Tilbrook
church. A *recently* dead body,' I added quickly.
'A very fresh corpse.' I hoped the operator

38

wouldn't take me for a hoaxer. 'Yes, that's Tilbrook St. George, three miles west of the A140 and five miles south of Mendlesett. My name's Ellie Hardwick. I'm the church architect. Yes, of course I can stay put. About fifteen minutes? As long as that? Okay. Yes, of course. Thanks.'

I rang off and looked at Edward Hartest. His astonishment and dismay were all that I could have asked for. Without a word he turned and began to run up the path to the church.

'Oy! Stop!' I called after him. 'Mr. Hartest, you shouldn't go in there! Not until the police arrive!'

He stopped and waited for me to catch up with him. 'Now listen! It's my church and if some clown's dumped a body in there, I've a right to know about it. If you're scared, you can wait outside.' He paused for a moment, looked at me speculatively and went on, 'On second thoughts, you're right. I'd be a fool to go blundering around in a crime scene without a witness so you'll have to be it. Come on!'

He tucked my arm firmly under his, partially as support but more, I believed, to stop me running off again, pushed open the door and marched me into the church. We set off to walk up the aisle, the strangest couple to undertake this walk together in the thousand years of its existence, I thought: middle-aged farmer, boots treading grass and earth up the

39

smooth red wilton and me, a Lego figure in the firm's green overalls and white plastic hard hat.

'The table tomb,' I whispered. 'She's laid out on the tomb. East end, south transept.'

He stood to gaze down at the scene which had held me spellbound moments before. I watched him closely. There was no mistaking his shock. He made the sign of the cross and went on looking, drinking in every detail. The shock melted into an expression of great sadness, sadness which burned away the irritation between us. It was clear the girl was known to him, possibly even well known.

'My God,' he muttered and again, shaking his head, 'My God!'

'Do you know her? Family?' I asked diffidently.

'Yes,' he said. 'Well, very nearly family. Let me present . . .' he gestured to the figures on the tomb, 'on the right, my ancestor, Sir John Hartest, first Baron Brancaster, and on the left, the mortal remains of the future Lady Brancaster, my son's fiancée. At least— she *was* the future Lady B. Not any more, it seems.'

I didn't know what to say. Polite phrases of condolence would have been out of place but he looked at me questioningly, expecting some sort of response.

'She's—she was—beautiful,' I said hesitantly. 'I think, no I'm sure, I've seen her somewhere before.'

'You'd have had to have been living on Mars not to recognise her!' he said surprisingly. 'This is Taro Tyler. She's staying with us.'

'Taro Tyler! Oh, yes, how stupid of me not to have seen it! It's just that . . . with her eyes closed . . . those wonderful green eyes . . . she's not so recognisable perhaps.'

Those remarkable eyes now growing milky under their stiffening lids—I'd seen them smiling out from the side of every bus in London, working their magic in countless up-market TV ads.

'Thank you. It's tactful of you to mention the eyes.'

Was there irony in what he said? I didn't doubt it and it made me angry. Her eyes, lovely though they were, had received less publicity than her famous breasts. Every man in the country knew their size and had run lustful eyes over them in the tabloid press. It shocked me that, however obliquely, he should be calling up the memory as we gazed in fascinated revulsion at the rust-fringed puncture in that glorious, money-spinning bosom.

'*On her left breast*
A mole cinque-spotted, like the crimson drops
I, the bottom of a cowslip,' he murmured but he wasn't really talking to me.

'Why do you suppose there's so little
41

blood?' I whispered, my eyes drawn to the red-brown patch encircling the dagger blade. 'There's just the merest trickle. Wouldn't you have expected a gush?'

'Not necessarily—with a heart wound. It's been expertly done. The dagger was placed with precision and left in the wound. It's a skilful job, a surgical job, not a wild, crazed stabbing. But perhaps it was just a lucky stroke?' He shrugged. 'At any rate I don't think we're going to find any blood-drenched overalls in the graveyard dustbin.'

'But how do you get a girl to just lie there while you plunge a dagger into her heart? Or was she killed somewhere else and the body brought here and arranged like this? And where on earth would you come by precisely the same dagger as the old man's got at his side? That's a misericorde, isn't it? It's all so deliberate! Look at her hair. It's been arranged to fall like that. Her dress—someone's folded it. And what would Taro Tyler be doing wearing an outfit like that anyway? It looks medieval!'

I gasped as the connection struck me.

'Only just caught on?' he asked acidly.

'She's meant to look like—be a replica of—the original figure . . . the figure I was supposed to be inspecting with you this morning.'

'I think so. Your firm sent some chaps last week to remove Sir John's alabaster wife,

Lady Aliénore. She was in need of remedial treatment. We called your boss who said, "Awfully sorry, I shall be away on holiday in Puglia but—tell you what—I'll send you my assistant. She's young and highly qualified, sound art historian. Pretty girl too,"' he added. 'Recognise yourself? I had the remains of the first Lady Brancaster placed over there in the corner on that tarpaulin.'

He nodded towards the bell tower and to an ordered pile of pale-gleaming fragments rising from which I could make out a single white hand pointing forlornly heaven-wards.

I had looked calmly enough at the dead girl but, unaccountably, the sight of the dismembered stone limbs made me shudder.

'I think I'm going to be sick,' I muttered and for a moment it seemed horribly likely.

'No you're not!' he said. 'Have a thought for the Suffolk Constabulary! They'll have quite enough bodily fluids to put under their microscopes without being distracted by extraneous and irrelevant contributions from the visiting architect. Pull yourself together, Miss . . . er . . .!'

He'd said it again! No one had told me to pull myself together since primary school. I breathed deeply, beginning sincerely to dislike Edward Hartest.

'Ellie, call me Ellie,' I said impatiently.

'Fine. And you might as well call me Edward. Now look here, Ellie, I want you to

43

note a few things before the police get here. I'm certain that we can rely on them to use the full range of their forensic techniques but . . .'

'I know what you're getting at. Not straightforward is it? It's as though someone's left a challenge. If it weren't such a gruesome thought I might even say—someone's playing a game.'

'Yes, and I have a feeling I may know the identity of this joker! Do you see, over there, just below the scrolled edge—don't touch it for God's sake!—there's a smudge.'

'A finger print,' I said firmly. 'In blood!'

My fingers may have strayed unconsciously to my camera because he looked down at me and glowered. 'Don't even think of it!' he said repressively. He paused, eyeing my Nikon. 'You haven't already, have you? I'm afraid I must insist you hand over the film.'

'Film?'

'You know what I mean!' He waved an imperious hand at my camera. 'Do whatever you have to do to disarm that contraption.'

The authoritative voice was one which was used to being obeyed.

'Give me one good reason why I should!'

'I'll give you two. You could sell the negative of this scene to the gutter press for thousands and the family can do without the publicity. Secondly, if you don't I shall take it out anyway and, clumsy as I am with modern equipment, I might well do your toy

44

irreparable damage.'

With a display of truculence, I slowly removed the memory card and handed it over.

'What on earth's this?'

'It's what we use instead of film in the twenty-first century. There's nothing on there but exterior shots of Mendlesett . . . crumbling buttresses and worm-eaten woodwork. Only of value to me. Still, if it'll keep your hands off my equipment, the sacrifice is worth it.'

We looked at each other in silence for a moment until outside in the real world, one by one, cars crunched to a halt.

*   *   *

A Detective Inspector Jennings accompanied by a detective sergeant and a uniformed officer marched aggressively in through the door and up the aisle. He made his way towards us, holding up his credentials for our inspection, unnecessarily it seemed as The Hon Edward greeted him with an easy, 'Oh, hallo there, Richard!'

After briefly establishing who I was and my role in the discovery of the body, the inspector courteously invited us to get out of the church by the fastest route and to avoid treading again on the carpet. I noticed that he spoke to Edward Hartest formally but with an underlying deference and I remembered—not only Honourable but also J.P.—Justice of the Peace, a local magistrate. This heir of an ancient family moved smoothly into action and, replying with just the right blend of formality and charm, informed the Inspector that we would leave the scene of crime clear for the investigating officers and go to await his questions in the comfort of the library at Tilbrook Hall where he trusted Richard would be able to join us later for coffee. Edward picked up my briefcase, put a chivalrous arm around my shoulders and led me out into the sunshine.

Through the thin cotton of my overalls I could feel the solicitous arm shaking perceptibly.

*   *   *

As we left, uniformed policemen were cordoning off the churchyard with plastic tape, one firmly standing his ground and denying access to an indignant, weather-beaten lady. 'Young man, kindly move aside. I always do the flowers on a Wednesday!'

'But not this Wednesday, I'm afraid, madam,' I heard him say cheerfully. 'Church closed to the public until further notice.'

A middle-aged figure, bespectacled and distinguished, climbed out of his Volvo, an assistant carrying his medical bag. The pathologist? 'Got a little local difficulty I hear, Edward?' he said, managing to sound both amused and concerned.

'Local, Gordon, but I' m not so sure about little,' said Edward.

'Am I the only outsider here?' I wondered resentfully.

*   *   *

The Hall was only five minutes walk from the church. A gable end was visible above the surrounding trees and the five shafted cluster of a chimney stack broke the skyline. Fifteenth century was my first impression. A fine house. A gracious and welcoming house. I was shown into the library and a tray of coffee was placed at my elbow while Edward went off to break the news of the death to his son Rupert, still abed, according to the housekeeper, and to his father, the current Lord Brancaster, up but feeling poorly.

I strolled around the library, admiring the ranks of leather-bound books, but finding not one I was tempted to take down and read. Fresh flowers in silver vases dotted the tables and a log fire smouldered in the grate of the stately fireplace. The latest model computer, perched almost apologetically on a table at the far side of the room was the only concession to the twenty-first century.

I passed the time taking from my briefcase the file on Tilbrook Church. Meticulously kept, the notes went back for thirty years. The fabric was in first class condition scrupulously maintained by the Hartest family. The damage to Aliénore had been caused by an overzealous Victorian insertion of iron cramps and I had been called in to advise on the restoration. Intrigued to see the original appearance of the tomb I spread out on the library table a set of black and white photographs we kept as a record in the file.

I looked and looked again at the pictures of the original Aliénore, intrigued and mystified. I compared them with the startling scene I had just witnessed and, unbelieving, I began to arrive at a shocking conclusion. And then there was the Latin inscription running round the tomb. This reinforced my disturbing theory. The words were an easily translatable, common enough formula until I got to the last word.

What I saw written there was a motive for murder. And it had been there, unnoticed, for nearly six hundred years.

*   *   *

I decided it would be a good idea to scramble out of my unglamorous overalls though the jeans and yellow T shirt this manoeuvre revealed were hardly more appropriate to the leather bindings, the gilded titles and the polished oak of these gracious surroundings. Even so, I was more suitably dressed than the young man who now staggered in through the doorway. Rupert Hartest looked every inch the bereaved fiancé. Stunned, inarticulate, dressed in a white bathrobe, his black hair flopping unbrushed and still damp from his shower, he stood and stared at me.

He was very good looking in a brooding dark way and very young. I guessed that he was probably in his mid twenties and a year or two younger than me. He joined me at the table and listened in silent horror to the story I had to tell him, dabbing his eyes with the trailing end of his bathrobe. When I fell silent he sniffed, and whispered gruffly, 'Oh, Taro! Consistent to the last! You silly little trollop!' He paused for a moment, smiled a crooked smile and added, 'But what an exit!'

Deeply puzzled, I pretended not to have heard and said, 'Your father thinks he knows who's responsible . . .'

'Theo Tindall,' he said bitterly, 'that's who he's got in his sights. The photographer. Taro's manager, friend, ex-partner and purveyor of strange substances to Taro and others— including myself.' He shook his head as though he could shake out memories. 'Hateful man! He was staying with us too, just for the week— at Taro's invitation of course. Perhaps I don't need to say that he's disappeared. Room's empty though his things are still lying around all over the floor. Mrs. Rose, our housekeeper, says he and Taro went out together in his car

49

early this morning at about seven o'clock.'

I told him about the bloody finger print on the tomb.

His relief was obvious. 'Well, they'll nail him then, no problem.' He paused for a moment, thoughtful, and then added, 'Funny though . . . what possible motive could there have been? He had every reason to keep Taro in good health. He made a lot of money out of her. He discovered her and flogged her talents to the media. Took a large cut of the proceeds. He didn't seem to resent her getting engaged to me—he introduced us in fact and with all the publicity she could whip up over the society wedding he, they, stood to make even more. Odd, that . . .'

The scene in the church was beginning to make sense in the context Rupert was setting out. The whole thing had been staged for a photographer's shoot. No wonder my own finger had twitched on the shutter! The display had been devised for exactly that reaction.

I decided to confide in him. 'Look, Rupert, would it be too distressing if I were to show you a photograph I took at the scene? The shot that this Theo had so carefully staged? Your father doesn't know I took it, by the way. He expressly told me not to.'

'I can imagine why! But, yes, Ellie, it would be distressing . . . though I think I ought to see it if you have it handy.'

I took the card from my pocket, a cable

50

from my briefcase and offered up my camera. I looked doubtfully at the computer and back at Rupert.

'I can manage,' he said. 'Allow me.'

In a few swift gestures he had transferred the image to his computer screen.

He studied the scene with stony face, running a delicate forefinger over the spilling golden hair on the screen. I fetched one of the black and white photos of the original tomb figures and we compared the two. The likeness was startling. Rupert made me go over again the details of the appearance of the corpse. 'The dagger,' he said finally, pointing, 'There's a real one in a trophy of arms in the drawing room, the twin of this. I looked in before I came to the library. It's missing. A misericorde, you're right. And I bet if I looked in the chest on the landing I'd find that a long white nightgown and a pair of white satin ballet shoes have gone missing too.'

'But do you think she changed into them willingly? Was Taro part of the impersonation, do you think?'

'Certain of it! Just the sort of off-beat humour she went in for. Bet it was all her idea. I can imagine what they were both up to! What a laugh! Dress up as the first Lady Brancaster and pose, with a lot of bosom showing of course, on the family tomb which somebody has conveniently cleared for them. Theo snaps away and flogs the result to . . . oh, any one

51

of a hundred papers. You can imagine the headlines! Blast them!'

'But wouldn't she have been a bit more circumspect . . . I mean . . . have held off from offending the ancient family she was about to marry into? Surely?'

Rupert snorted. 'She had no respect for that sort of thing. She refused to use or acknowledge Grandpa's title. She was the type who cheer when hereditary peers are kicked out of the House of Lords. I've always thought it was Taro and her sarcastic tongue that gave Grandfather his heart attack.'

'Is that possible?'

He grimaced at the memory. 'It happened at her first dinner here. She said something deliberately calculated to get up Grandfather's nose and then announced that she and I were engaged to be married and he'd better get used to hearing her opinions. She declared that she'd make every effort to talk me out of taking up the title when the time came. Who on earth cared about such things these days? And even if I did take it up she'd make sure any children we had were daughters so it would die out. Bluffing, of course, but the old chap's heard of designer babies and DNA and all that and I think he really believed she could do it. Poor old bloke sent for his doctor and went to his room. He hasn't come downstairs since. Doc says he's got a heart condition and has to avoid stress. He's over eighty now.

Seems a bit strange in these days perhaps,' Rupert looked at me, calculating, wondering whether he need explain, 'but he really is obsessed by—lost in—family history. Heraldry, pedigrees . . . His family motto . . . our family motto . . . is *Who dies, if Hartest live!*'

I must have looked bewildered because with an apologetic smile he said, 'I suppose it means: To hell with everyone else! Who cares—so long as the Hartests survive. Nice sentiment!'

Rupert's eye flicked to a photograph on the mantelpiece and I went over to look at it. Three generations of the Hartest men were lined up on the lawn, smiling at the camera.

'There you see, until the last few weeks Grandpa was always fighting fit—literally fighting fit! He was a commando and kept himself in shape. Tried to teach me and Dad all his skills. More successful with Dad—he was in the Coldstream.'

'Are you a soldier too?'

'I was for about eighteen months. Tried it for Grandpa's sake. Went through the motions. University then Sandhurst. I didn't impress them with my war-like spirit, I'm afraid. I got out. It wasn't for me. I'm more the arty type like my mother was. She died five years ago.'

'And in spite of all Taro had done, you were still prepared to go ahead with the marriage?' I couldn't hide my incredulity and disapproval.

His face softened. 'You never knew her, did you? It's hard for those who didn't know her to understand. She was magic . . . well, she magicked me anyway. She was a bit mad, ruthless even and she could be a ferocious little bitch (I knew it). But the magic made all that of no concern. Made! Christ! It continues to work! She's gone—but I can't believe it.

'I loved her. And there was another reason. She was pregnant. Not very, but enough to make us name an earlyish date.' He sighed. 'No illegitimate children were ever acknowledged in the Hartest family for six hundred years. Not going to start now, though Taro wouldn't have cared I suppose.'

He fell silent, deep in thought, and then he began to fidget. 'Look, Dad'll be down soon and he won't be amused to see me still in my bathrobe. He thinks I'm pretty dissolute . . . I'll just go upstairs and get kitted out. Stay here, I won't be a minute. Oh, and better turn that computer off.'

I was left alone but for the company of a Jacobean Hartest whose harsh white face under a black periwig stared down at me watchful, austere and calculating from its gilded frame. I felt a sadness so oppressive that I put my head in my hands and tried to force back tears. Two innocent lives had been lost on that marble slab this morning. The girl and her unborn child were unknown to me but I mourned them. And, underlying the sorrow,

54

was a barely understood suspicion of the Hartest men and their motives. I looked at my watch and wondered how much longer I would have to wait here. I found I really didn't want to have any further dealings with this family. Three generations of trained killers were loose in this house and one of them was ruthless enough to have got rid of an inconvenient little trollop. I looked again at the photograph of the table tomb, at the frozen features and flowing hair of the lovely Aliénore and I understood that an ancient tragedy had sent its echo on through the centuries to be replayed in front of my eyes this spring morning.

*　　　*　　　*

How soon could I get away from this place? I listened anxiously for the sound of a police car. My thoughts were redirected by Rupert. He slipped back into the room, smelling of herbs and wearing a fresh pair of jeans and a white tee shirt. He tapped a finger on one of the photographs of the Lady Aliénore.

'Always puzzled me this,' he said. 'I've spent hours in church on Sundays looking, enchanted, at this figure and there's something about her I've never understood. Dad says you're an art historian? Well, tell me, Ellie,' he indicated the flowing hairstyle of the stone image, 'in all the other table tombs I've seen the ladies have their hair gathered up into a head dress . . . Why is this one different?'

Should I tell him? Would he want to hear? I've never been able to keep knowledge to myself. 'That's the key to the whole mystery, Rupert,' I said. He looked genuinely at a loss so I went on, 'In these times it was the fashion for women to have their hair dressed and caught up in concealing coifs . . . if you were a respectable, married woman that is.'

'But Aliénore was all that! What are you trying to say?'

'That in those days this sumptuous spread of tresses was seen as the outward badge—the emblem if you like—of a common prostitute. Whoever put this here knew it and wanted succeeding generations to know it too. Sir John was announcing this to the world in sculpture. Vilifying his wife for eternity. An obscure but neat way of getting his own back for what he saw as his wife's shortcomings.'

'Interesting theory but a bit thin, I think. Impossible to read that much into a hairstyle!'

'Perhaps, but there's something else. Look here . . . and here . . .' I pointed to the inscription which ran around the sides of the tomb. 'Know any Latin, Rupert?'

'Enough,' he said. 'This at any rate—I've known it for years.' He started to translate the lines about Sir John, his date of death and age at death.

'It's the short statement about Aliénore that's important,' I said.

'Easy,' said Rupert. '*Hic iacet Alienora Iohannis Hartestis uxor.* That means Here Lies Aliénore, wife of John Hartest.'

'But that's not the end of the sentence. My firm is nothing if not thorough and back in the past someone must have thought he was not doing his job properly if he failed to check out the condition of the fourth side of the tomb.'

'But you can't see it. It's hidden—it's right up against a half height run of panelling.'

'As I said—we're thorough! Someone must have taken down a bit of the panelling to check for damp and observe the north face and he recorded what he saw on a photo—this one.'

'There's a bit more Latin,' said Rupert, surprised. 'But you've got me this time. I can't translate that.'

'I can,' I said slowly. 'It's a continuation of the inscription about Aliénore. The whole thing reads: *Hic iacet Alienora Iohannis Hartestis uxor et meretrix.* A slap in the face from beyond the grave.'

'Ellie—please stop showing off and tell me—what the hell does *et meretrix* mean?'

'It means "and harlot". It says, "Aliénore—wife and harlot." It means, Rupert, that Sir John considered his wife a—what did you say earlier?—a silly little trollop.'

*　　　*　　　*

We looked at each other steadily for a

57

moment. The fire crackled. Somewhere a clock struck eleven.

'What are you saying?' Rupert's voice was smooth and quiet.

'I'm saying that for some men—for some families—the idea of the purity of the line was very important. We'll never know whether your ancestor went as far as killing his lovely young wife—not unknown in those days—but the legitimacy of his offspring would have been vital to him. If Aliénore had been pregnant—inexplicably pregnant—and don't forget that these old knights were quite frequently away from home, for years on end sometimes, then horrors might ensue on his return. If he suspected that a child born to his wife was not his, he might well have murdered her. And the child.'

He listened without comment. We both knew I was really talking of Taro.

'Of course, we wouldn't have a problem nowadays,' he said confidently. 'DNA testing will sort out any paternity question.'

'After the baby's born,' I said, 'and by then it's too late if it's been accepted into a family which declares it never recognises illegitimate children.'

'You're saying that Taro was killed for a family reason. By *me*, in fact?'

Before I could answer Edward strode into the room. He had changed into a black jersey and light linen trousers. I stared. I had been

58

too quick to write him off as a waxed jacket and wellies type. He was slim and tall with stronger features but the same thick floppy hair as his son. An impressive man.

'Dad!' Rupert greeted him. 'How did he take it? Is he all right?'

'Of course. What would you expect? He took it well. His heart may be a bit dicky but there's nothing wrong with his mental equipment. Steady as ever. He grasped the situation at once.'

'Thank God for that! But Grandpa's going to need all his bottle if what your architect here has worked out turns out to be correct.' He threw a challenging smile at me. 'She's solved our crime! Move over Dick Jennings—you've been superseded by an art historian! And I grieve to tell you, Dad, it's down to you or me! Eeny, meeny, miney, mo, catch a killer by his toe! She's trying to decide which one of us did it! Come and look at this!'

Edward smiled bleakly and came to join us at the table. I wasn't amused. If my guesses were correct, with Rupert on one side and his father on the other, I was sitting shoulder to shoulder with a murderer. But on which side? A further chilling thought occurred to me—could they both be involved? At Edward's invitation I went haltingly through my theory again.

'A family thing. Yes, I believe you could be right, Ellie,' Edward said. 'But have you

59

considered that if Rupert is not the father of the child . . .' He turned to Rupert and said almost apologetically, 'Oh, come on, let's face it, Rupe, old son, you were out of your skull for most of the time till a few weeks ago and I don't think you had a clue about what was going on in Taro's life . . . then someone else is the father. That prat Theo what's his name? Imagine—Taro tells him she's marrying Rupert and giving up the modelling business. He's about to lose his cash cow and his prospective child. "Okay," he tells her, "I'll bow out of your life but how about one last shoot to send me on my way? A golden handshake from the glossies . . . I've had a terrific idea for a location . . . And we'll be able to stuff it up these Hartest prigs! Imagine their faces when they see the pics!" How does that sound? Revenge killing? Spite? Crime of passion?'

He was interrupted by Mrs. Rose who just had time to announce Detective Inspector Jennings when he came striding into the room. Settling down with a cup of coffee and placing his mobile phone importantly on the table in front of him along with his notepad, he smiled round at the small group, gathering our attention. My opinion of the police is not high but I thought that this inspector might just raise it a notch or two. He looked keen and energetic and clever. I just wished he'd been a little less impressed by the Hon Edward.

60

'I'll be needing your individual statements, of course, and when I've finished what I have to say, I'll send in an officer to take them. There have been developments,' he announced with satisfaction. His phone rang as though on cue and he snatched it up and listened eagerly.

'You've got him? Good lad! Where?' He looked at us and, involving us in his triumph, 'In his flat? You don't say! He must have burned some rubber down the A12! Flinging his passport into a bag? This guy's no Ronnie Biggs is he? Get the prints did you? What's his story then?' He listened avidly, occasionally chortling, occasionally cursing gently and finally switched off.

Stretching out his legs and leaning back in his chair, he announced, 'I'm pleased to say we've made an arrest! My London colleagues have picked up Theo Tindall in his Islington flat and charged him with the murder of Taro Tyler.' He looked at his watch. 'Has to be a record!' Then he added thoughtfully, 'Almost seems too easy . . .'

We didn't interrupt him and he went on, 'We got a statement from Mrs. Wentworth at Parsonage Cottage. Very good witness. She keeps an eye out for visitors to the church, in fact she unlocks at six a.m. and locks up again at dusk. She thought it was odd that tourists would come roaring up at seven so she took down their details, car make and number, the lot. Two people went into the church carrying a couple of bags. She noticed the girl was dressed like a bride and then she recognised them. Those guests at the Hall who'd giggled all the way through Matins last Sunday. They'd been sitting in a pew up by the table tomb. Gossip was that the girl was a model. Well that made sense didn't it? Catching the morning light for one of those fancy photos. Mrs. Wentworth went off watch. She noticed that the car drove away half an hour later, going rather fast but then young men always drive like that don't they?'

'We noticed a bloody finger print on the tomb,' Edward said.

'Yes, we've got it. That'll be checked by the morning but he admits it's his. Swears he didn't murder her but his story's a bit thin! Says they were all lined up for the shot, she spread out on the tomb in her draperies, when the light shifted and he decided he needed a different camera and a bit of extra equipment from the car. He nipped out to get it and came back minutes later to find her dead. Denies taking the dagger to the church as part of the props and says the first he'd seen of it was the handle sticking out of the body. Says he tried to pull it out. People will do that! Can't seem to keep their hands off. Yanking the knife out kills the poor bugger they're trying to save as often as not . . . Well, if he did there'll be prints there as well.'

He paused again, thinking aloud. 'Neat, all sewn up, you might say. Yes, very neat and tidy . . . Anyway, he got some blood on his hand, panicked and ran off. Says he felt sure someone was in the church watching him and he thought he might be next for the chop. It all sounds so feeble, it could just be the truth . . . We'll need a motive, of course. If he did take the dagger from the Hall, then it was premeditated. Her manager, I understand? I'd feel easier if we knew why he'd done it. Wondered if you . . .?'

'Oh, yes, Richard. I think we can supply you with a motive,' said Edward smoothly.

*   *   *

The sound of a shot from the floor above wiped the triumph from his face.

My three companions all jumped to their feet looking at each other with total dismay.

Rupert was the first to move. 'Grandpa!' he yelled. 'That's from Grandpa's room!'

He started to the door. Edward and the inspector ran after him. I lingered behind just long enough to cast an eye over the inspector's belongings abandoned on the table. There was something I had to find out without anyone noticing. Shifty but determined, I picked up his mobile and, one eye on the door, began to scroll through his phone book. I told myself what I was doing was in the interests of justice—and self-preservation.

I scrambled after the others, hurrying up the staircase and along a corridor. Rupert burst into the room at the end and we all gathered behind him, keeping to the doorway. Peering over Jennings' shoulder I could just make out the body of an old man wearing a camouflage-patterned sweater and dark cord trousers slumped across his desk under the window. A service revolver lay on the floor by his right hand. The wall to his left was spattered with blood. Edward put an arm around his son and hugged him, both men's faces white with shock.

Jennings went into action. 'Stay back,' he said unnecessarily. No one was trying to get close. He went to the desk and went through the automatic and superfluous gestures of checking the body for vital signs then abandoned this ritual and noticed the arrangement on the desk top. A large iron key was acting as paperweight for a single sheet of hand-written paper. He looked at it and waved to Edward. 'Come and have a look at this,' he said quietly. 'Looks like a suicide note and it's addressed to you. Edward.'

Edward went forward and began to read aloud. He needn't have done this and I wondered why he was involving us all in this way. More showmanship? I thought so.

'My dearest Eddie, forgive me. I killed that friend of Rupert's. Woman was a strumpet and did not deserve the honour he was about to bestow on her. I came down for a night-cap late last night and heard her planning—with that appalling photographer chap who's been infesting the place—to defile the family tomb. Couldn't have that. Made my preparations. I got to the church before them and let myself in through the vestry door on the north side using this old key. No one saw me. I hid and when the chap left the church to fetch something from his car I stabbed the girl with the dagger I'd taken from the display in the drawing room. I waited with the intention of terminating his miserable existence as well—I meant to snap his rabbit neck—but he was off like a flash. I couldn't have caught him. I'm a bit decrepit these days but not as bad as I've been making out. In fact, I was faking my condition. I took to my room to avoid meeting this dreadful pair of limpets. In any case— it occurred to me that he was more useful to us alive—he'd make a jolly useful suspect, damn his hide! I trust Rupert will learn from this fiasco and one day he'll be able to find a decent girl. God bless you both. Who dies? Eh?'

As he read I looked around the room, anywhere but at the poor, shattered body. I took in the military neatness of his arrangements, the bed already made, the books lined up on his bedside table. The only untidy item in the room was a pair of pyjamas lying in a crumpled heap on the bed. A discordant note in this precisely organised room. Fearful of what I might find, unnoticed by the others, I edged nearer, put out a hand and touched them. I looked at the carafe of water and the bottle of pills on the bedside table and I moved around until I could see the label and the contents.

What I saw confirmed all my fears.

*　　*　　*

Hours later after a sketchy lunch in which no one was interested and a tea tray in the library which seemed to have become the operations room, the police had finally left. Statements had been taken, frantic phone calls made, ambulances, police vehicles, pathologist and undertaker had gone about their business and, somewhere in the Islington nick I hoped that someone had thought to release Theo Tindall.

*　　*　　*

It had been a long, weary and sickening day but finally a weight seemed to have lifted from Edward Hartest. He poured me a glass of sherry, having, on one pretext or another, prevented my leaving for the last two hours. 'Nonsense! Not in the way at all! I can never apologise enough for dragging you into such a grisly family scene but we've both been glad you were here. Kept us in touch with sanity in an increasingly mad scenario, you might say. And you were right, you see, Ellie, about the motive. Purity of the line. It meant a lot to my father.' He fell silent, plunging into painful thought. Recovering himself he said, more brightly, 'Ellie? Now that's short for Eleanor isn't it? And funnily enough, that's the modern spelling of Aliénore. Did you know that? Your surname's Hardwick? One of the Norfolk Hardwicks are you? Then your family are apple growers? You must know a good deal about apples?'

Suspicious and disturbed by his change of tone, I admitted that I did.

'Look, before you go, you must take a stroll in the orchard with me. The blossom's wonderful at the moment. We've got some very special old strains that might interest an expert.'

The thought of wandering under the trees in the scented twilight with the handsome dark lord was making my knees quiver. I tried to fix an interested smile and appear relaxed but all my senses were screaming a warning.

For two men who'd just suffered a double bereavement, Rupert and Edward were charming hosts. But it was more than noblesse obliging them to put on a good show—they were hanging on to me because my presence was a necessary buffer between them. When I had gone they would be left alone with each other, with recriminations perhaps and with much sorrow. For the moment I presented them with the need to behave normally. I got to my feet, picking up my bag. I had to take my leave carefully, raising no suspicion that I knew a huge injustice had been done and that one of these charming men was a killer, a killer with the deaths of a young girl, her unborn child and an innocent old man on his conscience.

Neither man had an alibi for the time of the murder. Rupert was thought to have been in bed and had made a rather stagey appearance in his bathrobe at ten thirty. Edward had told the police in his straightforward way that, as usual, he'd been working by himself in the fields since six o'clock. If the Inspector cared to ask, any one of what he called his chaps might be able to state that they'd spotted him out in the pightle, mending the tractor. Somehow I thought his chaps might be queuing up, tugging their forelocks, to do just that.

The killer was probably trying to calculate how much I had worked out for myself, assessing from my behaviour how urgently I was trying to get away to raise the alarm, perhaps even working on a scheme to ensure my discretion—or my silence.

Rupert scrambled to his feet and firmly took my bag. 'No, it's all right, Dad! The last thing Ellie wants is to go wandering round a

68

damp orchard at this time of night. We're not all apple freaks you know! I'll walk you to your car, Ellie . . . No, I insist! It's a bit dark down the lane now,' he said. 'You left it in front of the church, didn't you?'

And we set off together to walk down the tree-lined driveway to the church. He took my hand and held it tightly with what might have been interpreted as friendly concern.

Distantly, the reassuring sound of the blue and white plastic ribbons outlining the crime scene flapping in the evening breeze was reaching my ears. We crunched on in silence down the gravel. Not much further to go. My hand curled round my car keys in the right hand pocket of my jeans. Fifty yards.

At the bottom of the drive, Rupert abruptly put down my bag, pulled me into the deep shadow of a lime tree, turned to face me and put two hands on my shoulders. 'You know don't you?' he said.

I shivered under his hands. 'Yes, I do,' I said defiantly.

'And I want to know what you're proposing to do about it.'

Keeping my voice level and unconcerned I said, 'Nothing. That's what I'm proposing to do. Who would listen to me in the face of so much evidence pointing so convincingly in a different direction? You've said it, Rupert— or was it your father?—It's a family thing. You can sort it out between you.'

69

'How did you guess?'

'It was no guess! Sharp observation and intelligent deduction!' I couldn't let him intimidate me. I looked anxiously down the lane, trying to make out the outline of my old Golf. Could I outrun him if he got angry? Probably not.

'It was the pills that gave it away.' I spoke with confidence. I think I even managed a flourish. No one ever attacked Miss Marple in the middle of one of her explanations. And somehow this felt like a dénouement.

'Pills, Ellie? What do you mean?'

'In your grandfather's room. All that stuff about his bad heart and being room bound—no one considered he could have done the killing but then, in his confession, he tells the world that it was all a bluff and, stiffening his old sinews, he does a commando-style exercise in the church for the sake of the family honour. Well, the police are happy they've worked out the bluff but they didn't think as far as a double bluff! The pill bottle by his bed, Rupert—it was half empty. He'd been taking whatever it was in there all right. And what was in there—I looked at the label—was a heavy duty heart disease prescription. My aunt had the same thing. So, your grandfather hadn't pretended—he was genuinely a heart attack victim and there's no way he could have done what he confessed to! He was owning up to a crime he didn't commit because he knew who had done it and was taking the blame for someone very dear to him. Paying the bill. For the family. Making sure that Hartest lives if you like.' I added softly, 'Ensuring your future, Rupert.'

'I don't know what to say. What can I do?' He seemed suddenly helpless and disarmingly childlike. 'I thought you'd worked it all out. Could be a bit of a problem . . .'

He thought for a moment and went on: 'You know he's mad, don't you?' he said. 'You'd have to be a bit mad, wouldn't you to kill like that and be prepared to let an innocent man—two innocent men—take the blame?'

I considered this. 'No, I don't think so. Just very focused and pitiless. You and I couldn't do it Rupert—we're the arty type remember. But your father could—and did. Who dies? Well, Theo Tindall for a start was a sacrificial victim. He was thrown to the wolves. But, just in case the wolves weren't having any—and that bright Jennings was beginning to make dissatisfied noises—even his own father . . . Yes, I think so . . . He told his father exactly what he'd done and, using this knowledge, the old chap cobbled together a convincing confession. He didn't have much time. He wanted to fire the shot while Jennings was in the house, I'd guess—a police witness right there on the spot. He hurried to write the confession and then thought of a corroborative detail—he got out of his pyjamas, leaving

71

them in a heap, and dressed himself up in camouflage gear to make it look credible. But his pyjamas were still warm. He'd taken them off only a few minutes before he shot himself.'

I paused for a moment, mind racing. 'Would we be really mean, Rupert, if the thought crossed our minds that this was just what Edward calculated would happen? You know your father best—would he consider it no more than right and just that the old should sacrifice themselves for the young? I think that was in his philosophy and your grandfather's. They saw you couldn't find the strength to extricate yourself from what they considered an impossible situation and they acted. I can't say they were doing it for you because in their thinking the individual is only a link in a chain. They were making sure a six hundred year old chain wasn't broken.

'So that's what I come down to?' said Rupert unhappily. 'The weak link in the family chain! Thanks!'

Lightening my tone I went on, 'As for what you do now . . . well, you go out and find yourself a respectable girl with a good name, marry her, have several male offspring and you'll find he need never kill again.'

I spoke flippantly but his reaction was unexpected.

Rupert smiled a devastating smile, reached out a forefinger and gently stroked my cheek. 'Eleanor's a good name,' he murmured, leaning closer.

I managed to fight down a shudder of fear and even retained my slight dismissive smile. The two Hartest men might have different methods of ensuring my silence—murder or matrimony—and on the whole, Rupert's method was to be preferred, but in the end they shared the same compelling family motto and the next victim they had in their sights was me. 'Who dies?' It wasn't going to be me. I'd decided some hours ago to adopt a motto of my own. *Semper vigilans* wouldn't be bad, I'd thought ... always on the alert.

'And I think you're very attractive,' Rupert was whispering, his eyes gleaming like a spaniel's in the moonlight. 'It didn't take me long to work out that you were a strong girl, dependable, discreet ...'

I swallowed and in what I imagined to be a light and friendly tone I agreed with him. 'Oh, yes. All that. And clever too. It didn't take *me* long to work out that the name Eleanor in conjunction with the name Hartest is not a lucky combination! It gets carved on tombstones. Prematurely. Goodbye, Rupert. I'll keep an interested eye on the announcements column in the *Times*! I may even turn up at your wedding!'

Truce? Stand off? Too soft for Sandhurst? He wasn't the ruthless tactician his father was. He let me get away.

*   *   *

Back in the safety of my Golf, I turned the key with shaking hand and said a quick prayer when the engine started. Two miles away on the busy, brightly-lit forecourt of a filling station I stopped and took out my phone.

I dialled a number I'd scribbled down in the library on the inside of my wrist.

'Inspector Jennings?' I said. 'Sorry to ring you at home. Ellie Hardwick here. You know—we met at the church this morning . . . I'm afraid I have to tell you something you really won't want to hear . . .'

A THREATENED SPECIES

An Ellie Hardwick, Architect, Mystery.

I knew I shouldn't be doing this.

It was against all the firm's safety rules to enter a deserted church, at dusk, alone.

I was due to inspect the place the next day anyway, in the morning sunshine and the comforting presence of Ben Crabtree, the county of Suffolk's best ancient buildings contractor. So why couldn't I wait? Why was I creeping, ankle-deep in rotting wilton, along the aisle, jumping at every owl hoot and mouse rustle, torch in one hand, mobile phone in the other and the firm's hard hat on my head?

I'm a romantic, I suppose, and I love old buildings in all their different moods. I'd come to catch what might well be the grace notes of the splendour of All Souls, adrift in the fields outside the village of Crowden. It would be my five-year survey tomorrow that would sign the death warrant for this once-lovely building. It had been disused for years and the grants of money, never generous enough, had finally run out. The fabric was considered dangerous and it was inevitable that the bulldozers would roll. The only people vocal in its support were the Bat Group.

'But the pipistrelles!' they shrieked. 'They're

a protected species! Their habitat must not be demolished!'

'I've nothing against bats but I'd like to slap a closing order on their support groups!' I'd said to my boss when he handed me the church file with a warning. 'The Barmy Bat Army! That chairman of theirs! Lady What's 'Er Name . . .'

'Frampton,' supplied Charles. 'Laetitia Frampton.'

'Yes. Well, the lady gave me a very bad time over Mendlesett Church last year. I don't fancy another encounter just yet.'

'Oh, I don't know,' said Charles vaguely. 'I suppose the bats are worth saving. Never seen it myself but they do say the twilight flight of bats out of the church tower is one of the sights of Suffolk. They were still firmly in place when the last quinquennial inspection was done. Byam did it. Now *he* seemed to get on all right with the lovely Laetitia.' Charles rolled his eyes in a meaningful way. 'They spent quite some time observing the habits of our leather-winged friends in remote church towers all over the county, I seem to remember.'

'Byam? Byam who? Or should I say who Byam?'

'Ah . . . He left a couple of years before you arrived. So that'll be five years, give or take . . . Byam Somersham. Damn good architect . . . Good looking chap as well. Women round here seem to go for that dark, romantic look.'

76

He grinned, remembering. 'I never could persuade him to get rid of his piratical earing.' Charles tugged absent-mindedly at his left ear. 'Can't say the infringement of the House Style put off the lady clients though—there was always a waiting list for Byam. Pity he . . . but . . . Anyway, he left the country soon after this bit of work. Went to Spain . . . or was it Portugal?'

I'd been passing on the main road on the way home from a job in Norfolk and had suddenly caught sight of the tower of All Souls silhouetted against a darkening blood-red sky, streaked with saffron. One of those vivid late-summer sunsets we get just after harvesting. I couldn't resist. 'I'll just poke my head inside,' I told myself, turning into the driveway to the church. 'Might be in time to witness the twilight flight of the pipistrelles.' I watched the shadows lengthen under the stand of ancient oaks which gathered protectively, still wearing their dark leaf canopy, around the secluded stones but no bats flew out to greet me.

And here I was, giving in to temptation and enjoying the guilty frisson of going against all common sense and Charles' firm rules. I paused to sit on the back row of pews to say a silent prayer for the building as I always did and then went on down the aisle, sorrowful for the poor condition of the fabric, the boarded-up windows, the cracked masonry, the water stains running down the plastered walls.

And then I heard it. A trickle of sound at first, growing louder and more insistent: the chirping, twittering, agitated noise that bats make when they're about to take off. I decided to find out where they were roosting. If I was quick enough, I might actually see them emerge from their holes in the rafters or window dressings. I hurried silently back down the nave to the bell tower. The door was swinging open. Checking the state of the staircase with my torch, I was relieved to see that this bit of the fabric at least had been replaced since the middle ages. It was of stout steel. Not pretty, but a tug and a kick convinced me it was firm. I began to climb. I planned to go as far as the first floor but no further than that. Too risky. Up on the platform, the noise of the bats was louder. Would the light of my torch disturb them? I shone it anyway over the floor. Stout oak floorboards, complete, and no holes down which I might stick a foot. There were hundreds of bats tuning up in the woodwork all around me and, I guessed in the very top floor above my head, thousands more. Not too late, then.

I shone the torch upwards from my feet. No staircase to the top floor. A very old oak ladder reached upwards to the trapdoor giving access to the bell tower. I ran the beam along it to check its condition. There was no chance I would climb that tonight but if it was obviously rickety I would ask Ben to bring a ladder with him tomorrow and impress him with my forethought.

Looking up, I became aware of a darker shadow amongst the shadows of the raftered roof. As I watched, it moved gently with a sudden gust of wind through a broken pane.

I leaned against the ladder to steady myself, unable to look away.

Above my head a huge black shape was suspended, life-sized, vampire-like. A stiff cape flapped in another gust. With a mew of fear audible even over the noise of the bats, I held my torch in both hands, lighting up the horror dangling above my head. Life-sized, yes, because this thing had once been human and alive. Legs and feet hung from the cloak, arms reached upwards, truncated, caught under the heavy trap-door. I forced myself to light the face. This was no pallid, bloodstained Dracula mask of horror films but—no less terrifying to me—I saw leathery features which might have lain, undiscovered for millennia, in an Egyptian sarcophagus or been hauled, as brown as the enveloping earth, from the depths of a peat bog.

I gulped and, as people do when frightened out of their wits, I said something very silly, just to hear the human sound of my own voice. 'Byam Somersham? I see you still have your earring . . . Byam, can this possibly be you?'

At that moment, with a rush and a high-pitched whirring, the whole population of bats poured from holes in every part of the tower. They surged into the air, zipping and diving past me and I flapped at them in panic, groping my way back to the head of the stairs. I was grateful to hear the clang of my boots on the steel treads as I scrambled down. I ran out to my Golf and, still shaking, dialled up a number on my mobile phone.

'Inspector Jennings? I wonder if you remember me? It's Ellie Hardwick here. I'm at All Souls' Church near Crowden and something awful's happened!'

Richard Jennings of the Eastern Counties CID groaned. 'I'm just going off duty and I don't want to hear this. What *is* it with you and churches? Oh, go on, then . . .'

He listened silently as I burbled on, ending dramatically with, 'Inspector . . . it's every architect's nightmare—getting themselves caught up in one of those trap doors! In a deserted church . . . no one to hear you scream . . . your phone's in your pocket and you can't get to it . . .' And, with an increasing hysteria I didn't like to hear: 'And you know no one's going to come near the building for another five years! It's Byam Somersham, isn't it?'

'Calm down and I'll get straight out to you,' said Jennings. 'Don't move from your car! Have you got a flask of coffee in there? Good. Keep some for me. Ten minutes.'

Cocooned in the lights of my car with an

up-beat jazz album playing and the windows fogging over with coffee fumes, I managed to get my teeth to unclench and my hands to stop trembling by the time the police car drew up. The inspector was by himself. He slid into the passenger seat, a large, masculine presence, took my cup from me and drained my coffee. He listened again to my story, nodding quietly.

Finally, 'I've been on the phone with headquarters on the way here,' he said. 'Spoke to someone in Missing Persons. It's looking most unlikely that this is your bloke. Somersham was indeed reported to them nearly five years ago. By his wife. But then she had to withdraw the notice because he turned up in Spain.' He paused for a moment, thoughtful. 'His car was found abandoned at Stansted airport. And he sent her a postcard on her birthday from Barcelona. He's sent one every year since he went off. CID checked. Date stamped in Spain. Certified husband's handwriting. A constable was actually on hand at the letter box to intercept one on delivery. At the lady's request. So that was that. No case. We'll have to look further. Earring, you say? Useful but plenty of fellers have them. I blame Johnny Depp. Floating cloak on the body? Ecclesiastical gear? What's the odds that a trendy vicar's gone missing lately, wearing one of those what do you call-ems?'

'Surplice? No, it's much shorter than that. Like . . . an old-fashioned policeman's cape ...'

'Eh? Good Lord!' said Jennings.

* * *

The inspector's torch was more powerful than
mine but I stayed as close to him as I could
without inviting comment.

'You don't have to do this, you know,' he
said when we reached the ladder. 'Leave it to
me.'

'I'm coming with you,' I said and began to
climb after him. 'Don't worry. I won't touch
anything I haven't already touched.'

We stood together gazing in silence at the
corpse. The brighter light of the police torch
revealed further horrors. Now I saw that the
dead face was even more appalling than I'd
guessed from my first startled look. It didn't
have the dreamy, at-rest quality of a bog-burial
or a Pharaoh: the eyes had been picked out
long ago by the carrion crows that haunted
the fields around and accusing black holes
were trained down on us; the shoulders were
stained with trailing white patches of pigeon
droppings. It had the macabre force of a
medieval execution, the look of a pirate's body
left to rot away on the Thames Embankment.

And that was odd, I thought.

And not the only odd detail. 'Look at his
shoes,' I whispered. 'Under all that dust those
are smart shoes, practically unworn. He didn't

walk three miles in those. He drove here. So, if this is Byam, who took his car to the airport and why didn't they come forward when he disappeared?' I shuddered at the implication.

Jennings put an arm protectively around my shoulders and I didn't shrug it away. I'd noticed that, in spite of its strength, the arm was quivering. I think he was glad of my company.

Half an hour later several urgent phone calls had produced a squad of professionals and I had lost the inspector to the well-oiled police machine as it took over, reducing the gothic horror of the setting to an arc-lamp-illuminated, plastic-taped, sanitised crime scene.

He paused by my car to say, 'You can go home now, Ellie, and I'll take your statement in the morning. Probably no more than a grisly accident we think but I'll call by your office at—say—nine? You'll have to put off your survey for a while, of course. Oh, your first guess was right, by the way. His hard hat's abandoned in the upper tower . . . wallet in his pocket had his driving licence and cards in it . . . It *was* Byam Somersham.'

*   *   *

By the time Ben Crabtree arrived to pick me up at the office I'd spent an hour studying the Crowden file. Richard Jennings had given me his automatic 'just leave it to the experts' speech but I was hardly listening. And in this field I counted myself an expert anyway. Ben hurried in, stunned and excited in equal measures by the brief outline I'd given him on the phone. After a few minutes of, 'Corst, blast! Who'd ever a thought it? So the old devil got his comeuppance! That trap's lined with ten pound lead, did you know that, Ellie? Accident waiting to happen! Poor old sod, though . . . awful way to go . . .' we settled down, file open on the desk between us, coffee mugs at elbow, to a gossipy discussion of the dead architect and his work. Strangely, Ben had most to say about the man himself.

His broad, honest Suffolk face clouded and he looked at me shiftily. 'Don't want to speak ill of the dead but . . . he were a right lot of no good, yon chap, Ellie. Fair architect—no denying *that*—but no good to the firm or any firm for that matter. We all said it when he went off—"Good riddance!"'

'That's a bit harsh, Ben? Why do you say that? Oh, come on, you can't leave it there!'

'Not to be trusted with the . . . er . . . female clients, shall I say?' he finally confided.

'Really! Attractive man was he?'

'Oh, yers, I'll say. Even *I* could see it!'

This was quite an admission from the aggressively masculine Ben. And as far as he was prepared to go. Suffolk people are nothing

84

if not discreet and unjudgmental and I was going to hear no more gossip from Ben.

Not so with Charles though. Hurrying through the office at that moment, he hesitated, picking up his bag. 'Attractive, you say? Byam? Yes, but it was his manner more than anything. He'd look at a woman—very long eyelashes he had, I remember—as if she was the only woman in the world and, do you know, at that moment he very likely thought so . . . And he could make 'em laugh. He'd have made *you* laugh, Ellie. You'd be surprised how many female clients suddenly decided to splash out on an extension so long as *he* was the architect in charge! I must say—he certainly brought the work in!'

Charles carried on, oblivious of our disapproval, 'Vain bloke though! Lord, how the man fancied himself! Snappy dresser and always wore a suit to work. But that cloak! Used to whisk about in it something sickening! He thought it made him look dashing—and the trouble is—it damned-well did! While the rest of us were muddling about on mucky sites in plastic Andy-Pandy suits for protection, he'd be swishing about looking like some sort of super-hero. The blokes on site used to laugh but the women loved it because he could carry it off! Anyway, whatever he had, it worked.'

He looked thoughtful for a moment and added, 'No . . . they don't make them like that any more.'

'Sounds like a species we can well do without,' I said crisply. 'He had a wife hereabouts, didn't he?'

'Catherine. Poor Catherine. Lovely Catherine. Still lives in the village. No one could understand why she put up with him and his goings on. But she always maintained he'd come back. Showed everyone postcards she got from him in Spain every year. "It's just a question of time," she says. "He's working out there. He'll be back when he's made his reputation." Not that she couldn't have done well for herself, either. She's had a bloke in the background for years. Gentleman-farmer type. Scott. Have you heard of him?'

I nodded. Handsome, middle-aged and perpetually broke, Tony Scott was quite a figure in the village. A single man since his divorce, he was rumoured to be paying out large alimony bills. I'd never connected him with the artistic Catherine Somersham with her eyes always dreamily on the middle distance. I'd seen her at village street fairs, I'd even bought one of her paintings, but had never met her.

Charles went off with a cheery, 'Say hello to the Plod for me . . . sorry I can't stay, but it's you they want to see, Ellie.'

Ben and I turned to the quinquennial survey carefully typed and filed and I raised a question that had occurred to me even while gazing at the leathery corpse. 'Look, I don't

86

know much about the state of dead bodies and no doubt the pathologist will have answers but, Ben, how do you think it could have been preserved like that for five years? Didn't putrefaction occur? You were the appointed builder at the time, I see, can you remember what the weather was like that summer?'

Ben's jaw dropped and he began to stir excitedly. 'That were hot. Days and days of heat. Best harvest for years, they say. And the autumn, the same. Do you think he might have been . . . well . . . kippered? Swinging about up there like an Orford smokie?'

'Could be. We'll ask Jennings when he arrives. But something else puzzled me, Ben . . . I'd have expected the body to have . . . um . . . fallen apart . . . been eaten away by insects. Wouldn't you?'

Ben considered for a moment. 'Look on page one, there should be something about pre-existing conditions . . . there—look.'

His splayed thumb indicated a paragraph and I read, '". . . extensive anti-infestation treatment carried out on all woodwork . . . insecticidal fluids" . . . Mmm . . . Heavy duty stuff. And the tower was sprayed. Small space—Byam prudently says he put the inspection off for a couple of days to allow the fumes to dissipate. I see. Are you thinking that any winged creatures that might have been interested in a body would have been knocked cold by the treatment?'

'It's possible, I'd have thought.'

There was a screech of gravel outside and Jennings strode into the office. He looked refreshed this morning and as brisk and bright as I remembered. He'd never met Ben before and I introduced the two men, explaining the builder's role in the Byam Somersham saga.

'. . . So, accidental death is what it seems to have been. A cracked skull caused instant death. He didn't suffer, Ellie,' the inspector was concerned to tell me. 'It looks as though he was coming down from the upper bell tower (though what the hell he was doing up there when the survey job was complete, I've no idea), missed his footing on the ladder and dropped the trap he was holding up over his head. It crashed down—did you know it was lead-lined?—of course you did—sorry. It bashed in the back and top of his head . . . here . . .' He picked up a file and demonstrated on Ben's head. 'Killed him at once and trapped his arms which were still extended over the lip of the hole.'

'We were wondering why the body didn't disintegrate and drop?' I said tentatively. 'In fact we've had some ideas.'

'To start with the most obvious thing—his suit was of very good quality, a light summer fabric but strong enough to sustain the weight of his body until it . . . well until we found it. To go on—we think putrefaction didn't occur because of the exceptional weather . . .'

'All those hot harvest days and it was well ventilated up there. Not one of those louvred windows is intact. "Kippered" is what Ben's saying.'

'Right. Yes. Well done.' He fished about in his briefcase and produced an e-mail print-out. 'Forensic entomologists—that's grub experts to you—are a bit puzzled though,' he said. 'This is just a preliminary statement—work could take days—but they're not able to find a great deal . . .'

'Ah. We think we can help you there!' Ben and I exchanged smug looks.

*   *   *

After Ben left, Jennings 'you'd better call me Richard', stayed on for a second cup of coffee. There was an uneasiness about him and I sensed that he still had questions. He didn't know whether to grill me in his role of interrogator or chat to me as a helpful assistant so I made it easy for him by launching into a few questions of my own.

'What was he doing up there when the report was finished and had been handed in for typing? Look here. Charles is very old-fashioned and doesn't yet quite trust modern technology. Oh, it's all on computer but he keeps the original dictated tapes just in case. Someone told him a bolt of lightning can have a dire effect on your hard-drive, since when it's been belt and braces.' I showed him a plastic bag which had been filed next to the document. I took out the small Dictaphone cassette it contained. 'I've checked it and you should perhaps have this but it's nothing more than the architect's survey. This is what may be important.' I peeled the small pink post-it note from the back of the cassette. 'It says "Bats! A.S.Ch. 8 p.m." He'd forgotten to inspect the bat accommodation. No reference to it in the body of the report. I think he probably went back as an afterthought to check up on the colony.'

'A.S.?'

'All Souls, the name of the church.'

'Of course. I'd better take those. Yes, thanks, Ellie. This all begins to fall into place. Except . . .'

'Those postcards to his wife? He can't have sent them. Who did? Is Catherine lying? What's going on?'

Jennings looked uncomfortable. 'I called on the widow last night and broke the news. She seemed distressed and horrified, I'd say. She stuck to her story about the cards . . . she keeps them in a row on her mantelpiece . . . And, as the authenticity was corroborated by the police—what can I say? It's all a bit awkward.'

Carefully, I said, 'I was thinking that, on behalf of the firm, I'd go along to see Catherine and express our condolences. A bunch of flowers, perhaps . . . What do you think, Richard?'

He grinned. 'I think that would be a good idea, Ellie. She teaches art at the local college. You'll probably find you have a lot in common.'

He turned to me as he left, his hand on the doorknob. 'Oh, if you get into a girlie chat with her, you might ask how she's going to spend the two hundred grand.'

'The two hundred grand?'

'Life insurance policy. She'd kept up the payments on her husband's life.' He paused and added thoughtfully, 'I always think it should be called a "death insurance policy" don't you?'

*   *   *

Catherine Somersham's greeting when she answered the door of the Old Mill House (conversion by Byam, I guessed) was warm. She even knew my name. I stood uncertainly on the doorstep, almost hidden behind a generous armful of white arum lilies.

'Come in! It is Ellie Hardwick, isn't it? You work with Charles? I'm just making some tea, will you have one? I won't say "Oh, you shouldn't have,"' she said gracefully, taking the lilies, 'because these are my favourites! Flowers *are* a sort of consolation, you know. And consolation is still, even after five years, much needed.'

While she went to put them in water I cast an eye around the living room and began to relax. I find anything minimal bleak and soulless and this room was the very opposite of minimal. It defied any label—I doubt Catherine was the kind of woman who cared about style—and she would probably have laughed if I'd suggested 'bohemian-chic'. It looked as though she had just collected into the room everything she admired or found comfortable. White sofas covered in coarse linen, wooden floors with Scandinavian rugs scattered over, books spilling over from shelves no longer equal to the task of housing them, white walls and everywhere, paintings, not all her own.

The conversation was surprisingly easy and led on from my genuine and enthusiastic comments on the painting I'd bought at the previous year's village art festival. She invited me to look at the other pictures on the walls and, while on my feet, I took the opportunity of strolling to the fireplace and admiring a bronze turn-of-the-century figure of a little dancer on the mantelpiece.

'No! It can't be a Degas, I know that! But it's the next best thing!'

'It's my great-grandmother.'

'She sculpted this?'

'Oh, no, sorry! She was the model. My great-grandfather did it,' she smiled.

I replaced it carefully, then hastily

began picking up the pile of postcards my manoeuvrings had scattered.

'Oh, dear!' I said in tones of mock horror. 'I wouldn't have taken you for an admirer of modern architecture . . . Spanish is it? Yes, these two are in Barcelona—a couple of Gaudi's best . . . then the Guggenheim Museum? The Sant Jordi Sports Palace? Not my favourite!'

'Nor mine,' she said easily. 'You can look at them if you want to. They're postcards Byam wrote.' She chewed her bottom lip for a moment, started to say something, sighed and then took the plunge. 'Ellie, I don't know what to do! Oh, do you mind my laying this on you? You'll wonder what on earth you've walked into! Bad enough that you had the shock of discovering the body . . . I feel as though I ought to apologize for him . . .'

I made encouraging noises and she went on haltingly, 'I've been fooling the police and now they know it. That nice inspector who came last night saw straight through the rubbish I was telling him. I'm not a good liar and I think he's pretty smart. What on earth can I say to them? I think they might be going to arrest me.'

'It's never a bad idea to tell the truth. That inspector you saw . . . Jennings? . . . he's half-way human. He would listen. I could give you his number if you like. Er . . . if it would help to rehearse it, see how it comes out, I'd gladly listen.'

I put on my receptive face. Not difficult as I was eager to hear and she responded by launching straight into her story.

'Five years ago when Byam disappeared I was left in limbo. Not a word. No note. He'd told me he was due some leave and he was going off for a few days by himself.' She glanced at me, her expression one of mixed defiance and shame. 'He did that occasionally. It was a price I paid . . . not happily but with a certain resignation, I suppose. But this time, none of the local ladies he'd had an affair with had gone missing in a companionable way.'

I looked at her, startled by her cold rationality.

Misinterpreting this she said hastily, 'Oh, *you* weren't . . . surely you . . .?'

'I never met the man,' I said firmly. 'I've only been working in the village three years.'

She took a photograph from a table and handed it to me. 'Meet him now,' she said quietly.

Even from the photograph the quality of the man leapt out. Not classically handsome, I thought, but I'd have turned in the street to look at him and speculate. Humorous, clever and interested is what he looked. It made last night's horror even more of an obscenity.

She took the photograph from me and sat holding it in her lap while she continued. 'Shortly after he went off I had a very good

94

reason to insist that he was still alive at least. I didn't want to be a widow and I didn't want to get a divorce. Two years before, we'd had a holiday in Spain and he'd bought and written out some postcards to friends and family and, as usual, he handed them to me to do the donkey-work—"Here, Cath, you'll remember the addresses. You can finish these off." Well, I rebelled. I didn't bother. They just came back home with us in the luggage. When I wanted to prove he was still alive, I remembered them. I took five or six of them over to a place I know in Spain and paid the hotel manager to post them to me on a given date, one a year. I put them each in a typed envelope. The police believed me because—well, why wouldn't they? I was saying what they wanted to hear. They must have been expecting me to try to prove he was *dead* because of the life insurance policy. But I needed my husband to be *alive*. For personal reasons.'

I was about to encourage her to enlarge on this when a Range Rover tore down the drive and parked in front of the house. A florid-faced man got out and hurried straight in. I noted with distaste that he had a bottle of champagne in the capacious pocket of his waxed jacket.

'Cathy! Cathy! Have you seen the news? Accidental death is what they're saying. Oh, who's this? Didn't realise you had company.' He looked around in a stagey way for my car.

'I walked. I work in the village.'

Catherine performed the introductions. 'My neighbour, Tony Scott.'

He stood glaring at me, willing me to leave. He was too large for the room, he'd left muddy prints on the shining floor, he smelled of diesel and he frightened me.

'Pleased to have met you Mr. Scott,' I lied with a sweet smile, 'but I must dash. Oh! Before I go! Nearly forgot, Catherine! The name of that new hairdresser . . . I like to support local initiatives, don't you?' I confided as I scribbled. 'Ask for Ricardo at Hairtique,' and added the inspector's mobile number.

Catherine smiled and nodded. 'Quite right, Ellie. Thank you for coming. I'll take your advice,' she said.

*   *   *

'It's so obvious why she's been deceiving people like that,' I said to Richard over a pint in the Angel that night. 'That Scott won't take no for an answer. She's been doing a Penelope.'

'A what?'

'Odysseus' wife! Repelling suitors by insisting her old man's still alive. Just taking an awfully long time to get back from the Trojan War. Penelope promised to marry one of the brigands who were after her fortune as soon as she'd finished a bit of weaving she

96

was doing. But at night she used to creep down and unpick what she'd done in the day time. Delaying tactics! Spun it out for years! Catherine's house must be worth a bob or two and now you tell me she's due to get a large sum from the insurance company. Tony's well known to be a bit short of cash . . . well—there you are. He's been putting pressure on her. Won't take no for an answer. You know the type. He worried me, Richard. He's a ball of pent-up violence. You're not to go near him.' I stopped abruptly and bit my lip.

'I'll be sure to keep my styling scissors ready in my back pocket,' he grinned.

'You'll just have to forgive her. All she's done is waste police time, isn't it?'

'I'll forgive your new friend if you'll do something for me,' he said mysteriously. 'Would you mind presenting yourself back at the scene tomorrow morning? Something I want to check on.'

*   *   *

'Never had the Law at my feet before.' I almost giggled with nerves at the sight of Richard's body, face down, on the dusty floor of the tower.

'Get on with it, Ellie,' he grumbled. 'My helmet's conveniently over there in the corner, you've coshed me on the head with one of those planks that litter the floor. I'm dead.

Now pull me towards the trapdoor.'

'Ankles or knees, Richard?'

'Take your pick.'

I tugged him by the ankles and to my surprise his body moved easily with the grain of the boards to the hatch. Gingerly I climbed half way down the ladder and pulled him after me. When I'd got him balanced with the weight of his upper body still bearing on the lip of the hole, steadying him firmly against the oak structure, I reached up and grasped the handle on the flap of the trapdoor which I'd propped open with a piece of planking on either side.

'I could do it Richard!' I gasped. 'If I push out one of the props and then the other, tugging you as it gives way, you're a dead man! Would be if you weren't already!'

He surged back to life and carefully moved the door out of reach.

'It could be done!' he said with satisfaction. 'And if *you* can do it, a 5' 4" female, anyone can. Let's get out of here, shall we?'

We went out into the sunshine and I flapped a hand at his jacket front, covered in dust and worse. He looked at it with interest.

'Probably splinters of oak floor boarding in there as well,' he said. 'Just like the ones we found down the front of Byam's cloak. We know he'd arranged a meeting here with someone. Had he lured some female up here with romantic intent? "Come up and

98

experience the twilight flight with me?"' he purred. He studied his jacket. 'Nice roll in the pigeon droppings? Amatory activity witnessed by a million swooping bats? Not the place *I'd* choose for an assignation.'

'Wouldn't work for me either,' I agreed. 'Have you thought, Richard, someone could have lured *Byam* here? He (could be she) sets up a meeting, gets someone to drop him off here, climbs the tower and kills him, leaves him dangling. He takes the keys from Byam's pocket—or perhaps they'd just been left in the car—and drives it away to the airport. Plenty of public transport back from there to anywhere in the county. With everyone's eyes on Spain, no one's going to look in a deserted church lost among the cornfields. He'd finished the job anyway and, according to his schedule, was supposed to be going on holiday.'

'The killer knew that the body would be found sooner or later but you could reasonably expect a body exposed like that to be judged a nasty accident as—for the moment—it *is*,' said Richard. 'And to show your faith in his survival and your innocence, you keep up the payments on his insurance policy and by waiting patiently—you know he'll be discovered in five years at the outside—you come into a tidy sum of money—and five years' rebate probably. They're in it together! Catherine and Scott.'

'Hold on! I'm not so sure,' I objected. I was

99

remembering the way Catherine had held her husband's photograph. Protectively. Lovingly. 'We're missing something here. Take me back to the office will you, Richard? There may be something in Byam's work records that throws up some information. Let's find out what else our local Don Giovanni was busy with.'

Charles was out on a job when we got back and we settled down with the dusty ledger from five years earlier which recorded the hours spent by each architect on each of his jobs. I pointed out Byam's record. It seemed he had quite a full programme. Ongoing repairs at five churches besides the quinquennial on All Souls. He had, typically, spent half a day at each, usually mornings. His afternoons had been spent on domestic projects: he'd been working on extensions to two private houses. In the record, one was named as 'Moat Farm Extns.' the other 'The Limes Extns.' Both were common names hereabouts.

'Out of county contractors, I see, on both jobs so no use asking Ben for his insights,' said Richard.

I remembered the cutting comment Charles had made about the ladies who ordered extensions and I wondered. I shared my suspicions with Richard.

'Names,' he said. 'How do we correlate these jobs with names of clients?'

'We look in the back. That's where Liz wrote down the accounts and payments before it all went on computer.'

We tracked down the two extension jobs and looked at the names of the clients.

'But isn't this . . .?' Richard started to say, recognising one of them. 'Oh, Good Lord! You don't imagine . . .? Surely not . . .?'

I stared at the page for a moment, taking in the meaning of the scene we had uncovered and, in an unthinking gesture of appalled rejection, I slammed the ledger shut.

'We can't leave it there,' said Richard. 'However much you might want to. But at the moment, all we've got is the suspicion of a scenario that could possibly have led to murder. It's not much. How can we find out more without committing ourselves?'

'I think I know how. Look at the dates. The work was started a year before Byam died. This lady was spinning it out? "While you're here, Byam, you might as well look at . . ." We get a lot of that. Can you imagine? It would have been under way by Christmas six years ago. I'll get the album.'

Every year Charles threw a party in mid-December for staff and clients and anyone who'd been involved with the firm in the past year. He enjoyed going around photographing the junketing and faithfully stuck his shots in an album. It was well-thumbed. I leafed back to the Christmas in question. Byam's last. Faces, familiar and unfamiliar, smiled happily or drunkenly at the camera.

'Look at this one, Ellie,' Richard murmured. 'Says it all really, don't you think?'

Byam was standing with his arm around a dark and flamboyantly good-looking woman. He was grinning at the photographer and waving a glass around. The woman was paying no attention to the man behind the camera; she only had eyes for Byam. I was a stranger to both of them but the relationship was clear. It seemed to be clear also to the man standing to the right of the pair, some feet away. He was not smiling. Head lowered, he was showing all the aggression and pent-up anger of a tormented bull. An anger directed straight at the unconcerned Byam.

Richard put a hand down the centre of the photograph, covering up the partying crowd in the background and concealing all but the three main players. The effect was astonishing. Revealed was a crime about to happen. 'Murderer, victim and motive, would you say? I think Byam extended himself a little too far on this occasion,' said Richard. 'Husband sees his wife the victim of a serial cuckolder . . . perhaps she's threatened to leave him and go off with the glamorous architect . . . so what does he do? Makes an appointment with the scallywag in a remote place and engineers his disappearance.'

'It didn't work, you know,' I added slowly. 'All in vain. The lady left her husband anyway, shortly after. He lives by himself.'

'A tragedy for all of them then. Makes you want to just slam the trapdoor back and cover the whole thing over,' said Richard surprisingly.

We sat together in silence, each assessing the evidence, hunting for a flaw, neither of us ready to take the next step. 'Oh, who's this?' said Richard, annoyed. 'Someone's just drawn up in a van. You've got a visitor.'

'It's Ben. You met him yesterday morning. I'm sure he can shed some light on this,' I said.

'Want me to leave?'

'You just stay put!'

Ben came striding in with his usual sunny confidence and stopped as he took in the books and the album open in front of us. Richard rose to his feet.

'Ah! The Christmas party book,' Ben said and he sat down in Richard's vacated chair to look at the photographs. 'You'll have figured it out then?' he added prosaically. His calloused forefinger gently traced the face of the dark-haired girl. 'You never met her, Ellie. Rachel. She was always too good for me. I knew that.' He swallowed and growled, 'She deserved better, but not him. No, never *him*! I couldn't stand by and watch her break her heart over that no-good poser. If he'd loved her back I don't think I'd have bothered.'

Richard stood uncertainly by. He seemed to be waiting for me to say something.

'You rang and arranged to meet him at

the tower, Ben? Mentioning some problem with the bats?' I suggested. 'The contractor,' I explained for Richard's benefit. 'Just about the only person in the world the architect would have agreed to see at that late hour at the end of a job. You got one of your blokes to drop you off and after you'd . . . afterwards . . . you drove off in Byam's car.'

'Story came out that he'd gone off to Spain. Broke my Rachel's heart. She didn't blame me. Why would she?—I never let on. But she pined for him. Never laughed again. Not like that.' He looked again with pain at the photograph. 'Nothing I could do. Seemed I'd killed her as well, in a way. She packed her bags and went off.'

Seeing Richard's shoulders tense he added wryly, 'Oh, nothing sinister! You'll find her at her mother's in Stowmarket. Well, shall we go, then? I always expected it would come out. But I reckoned I had five years. Five years to try to get her back. No chance now.'

He turned to me, tears glazing his eyes. 'Wouldn't be sorry to hear that damned church had been demolished. Was looking forward to swinging a half-ton ball at it myself! Let me know, Ellie, would you, when you've done the deed?'

A BLACK TIE AFFAIR

An Ellie Hardwick, Architect, story.

'Go on! You're 'aving a larf, Ellie! Evening suit? Me? Sorry, love. Look—if you wouldn't mind making that smart-casual, there's a bash on in town we could . . .'

I grunted with irritation and hung up as soon as I politely could. I crossed Jon Sanderson off my list. And his was the last name. My boss looked up from the elevation he was sketching and grinned at me across the office.

'Bad luck Ellie! What's the matter with the young men of the East of England? You can't tempt a single one of them to escort you to the social gathering of the season? They must be nuts!'

'Not a man under forty owns a black tie and dinner jacket any more. That's the matter. They've all given them away to Oxfam.' I waved an embossed invitation card at him and read:

Lord and Lady Redmayne request the
pleasure of the company of
Eleanor Hardwick
to celebrate with them their first year in
residence at Hallowes Hall.

'So far so good, but then it says along the

105

bottom: Dinner and dancing. Black tie. And I'm obviously not expected to turn up alone because there's a note from Alicia, paper-clipped to the card:

'Dear Ellie, Do so hope you can come and please bring the gentleman of your choice.'

'Well, that's not necessarily the same as a choice gentleman,' Charles quibbled. 'You'll have to spread your net wider and not be so fussy,' he added. 'And think of the firm. You did a splendid job on that old ruin of a house. The kitchen you designed is the most glamorous in Suffolk and there'll be hundreds of envious women there asking how it was done. Alicia's showing off the house but she's also showing off her architect. Go! And take some of our business cards with you. Leave them discreetly about the place. Like, on the kitchen table.'

I shuddered.

'That's an order not a suggestion. Only sorry I can't manage it myself. Now who can we think of? What about old Hamish Peabody—he can still cut a rug and his last procedure was a roaring success, they say.'

I wasn't listening. I was hunting glumly through my directory.

'Got it!' Charles shouted in triumph. 'Just the bloke! Young, handsome, energetic, polished . . . well, fairly polished . . . and in his line of work he's be bound to have some fancy suiting!'

'Johnny Depp's tied up that weekend,' I muttered.

'No, no! I'm talking about that police inspector who keeps hauling you in and out of trouble. What's his name . . .? Richard Something. Or was it Something Richard? Very traditional lot, the Filth. They have black tie do's all the time. Bet he's got just the thing.'

'Detective Inspector Richard Jennings?' I gave a grating laugh. 'We never managed to get it together, Charles, if you know what I mean. Both busy people, demanding bosses, bleepers calling us back to the office just as things get interesting. Haven't seen him for six months. Fast-Track-Man that he was, he's probably been promoted to the Met. by now. Still . . . good dancer and quite a charmer . . . I'll give it a go. You're not to interrupt.'

'Hello . . . is that Richard? Ellie Hardwick here.'

'Ellie? Oh, Ellie!'

I rushed on, embarrassed that he quite obviously had not been sitting by the phone expecting to hear from me for the last few months. 'Look, I was wondering if you owned a dinner suit and if you wouldn't mind putting it on to escort me to a glamorous event the Saturday after next? Pink champagne, jazz band, the cream of the county there . . .'

'I'll stop you right there and say—no, sorry, I have no such garment in my wardrobe.'

I must have sighed into the phone. He went

on: 'Is there a problem? Ellie? Is it important? Where is this event?'

'Hallowes Hall. The Redmaynes are celebrating a year's residence and I was to be paraded as their architect.'

There was a silence as he absorbed this, then: 'Hallowes Hall? This is the newly created peer of the realm—Lord Redmayne of Deben or some such—we're talking about, is it?'

'That one. Services to inner city regeneration and all that.'

'Huh! It used to be called property development in my day. Mmm. And you know these people well? I had no idea.'

'I only know them in a professional capacity but, as an architect, you do discover some intimate details—which I never disclose so don't ask.'

'Listen—my father has four evening outfits . . .'

'Four?'

'He never throws anything away and as his size increases he adds to his stock. And lends them out to me in emergencies. I've reached his size 2. Okay, Ellie, I'll borrow it and turn up in accordance with time and place you specify. Send me an e-mail. Schedule permitting, of course. You know what it's like.'

'You'll come? Great! But look, Richard, just in case you're called out at the last minute— book your father in for me would you? I'll be happy with a size four!'

'Not on your life!' I was reassured to hear his familiar chuckle. 'I wouldn't trust the old rogue within a hundred yards of you!'

*   *   *

I was more than content, I felt a stirring of excited anticipation as I glanced at my escort, guiding his old Saab skilfully down the rutted track between the cornfields towards the sound of jazzy music and laughter of a party well under way at the Hall ahead of us. DCI Jennings, done up in his number 2 outfit and smelling alluringly of something expensive and woody, was reassuringly correct.

'Don't worry, Ellie,' he said, catching an appraising glance, 'I won't let you down. You won't hear a clank of handcuffs coming from my back pocket and I won't put on my robot-copper's voice.'

He slowed to take in the long, low lines of the refurbished house and gave an appreciative whistle.

'Fifteenth century,' I told him. 'It's got the lot—king-posts in the roof, screens arches, panelled doors, even a priest's hole.' I looked at the steeply pitched roof with its gently undulating coverlet of plain tiles ranging in colour from a red so dark as to be almost black, through buff to white where the lime-torching on the underside showed through. 'So glad I managed to persuade Ronald not to strip the roof and re-tile. Those beauties are good for a few more years yet.'

The long front was plastered and colour-washed to a burnt orange, dark under the eaves, fading away to nothing at the brick plinth which ran round the house. As we watched, the setting sun, still undefeated on this late June evening, caught the leaded panes and sent back a dazzle of golden light. A double line of stout candles of medieval size wavering within their glass holders welcomed guests across the vast lawn to the marquee from where the sounds of jollity were coming.

Welcoming also and attentive was the pair of uniformed valets who took the car keys, exchanging masculine pleasantries with Jennings, and we set off across the grass towards the distant figures of Ronald and Alicia, standing ready to greet the last few guests. Richard, with an old-fashioned gesture took my arm and put it through his and, in my high heels, I found I was glad of the support.

Squeals of recognition, tuberose-scented air-kisses and manly hand-shakes welcomed us to the party and I was amused to see the interested look the dark-haired and willowy Alicia cast at the inspector. Amused also to hear him introduce himself to their host. 'How do you do, sir? Richard Jennings. Criminologist. Cambridge.'

'Oh, I say! D'you hear that, Alicia? A Cambridge academic. Another one! There's a professor of something or other poking about the place somewhere already . . . perhaps you know each other?'

'Medieval history,' Alicia hissed, suddenly witch-like in her intensity. 'Marcus is a historian. He's inspecting our cock's head hinges.'

Ronald rolled his eyes. 'Well, there you are,' he said happily. 'My good wife's latest enthusiasm! Cocks heads!' He added with a leer: 'Hinged or otherwise. And it's you I blame, Ellie, for getting her going. She's never at home these days—forever off on some historical workshop or tracking some luckless ancestor back through the rotting branches of her family tree. You must meet this chap, Marcus. If you can find him. Probably burrowed into the woodwork by now. Pink champagne? For you both? Or is the architect driving? Oh, before you move off, Ellie—do feel free to show your young man around the house. He'll be very impressed, I know!'

'What's that you're muttering, Richard?' I asked as we wandered over to the marquee clutching our champagne.

'Um . . . Nouveau-riche, arriviste, exploitative, bull-dozing chancer,' he said with a smile. 'That's what I was saying. And I was trying to be polite. If I were telling the whole truth I'd add—villain. How on earth did you get involved with these dodgy people, Ellie?'

'The usual way. Estate Agent's

recommendation. They pass our name to rich clients who need good guidance from a firm that knows the local property and isn't going to rip them off. The Redmaynes aren't generally known to be—what did you say?—something slanderous: crooks? In fact they're making quite a niche for themselves in local society.' I waved a hand around at the glittering crowd. Bare shoulders, supercilious glances, diamonds winking at the throat, over-loud laughter, flushed faces and male guffaws. 'A "Lord", however fresh the paint on his escutcheon, cuts some ice in this county. This is their new small pond. They want to be big fish in it and they've got the clout to do it. If they're at all uncertain they can hire people like me to advise them. Don't knock wealth, Richard, it creates a lot of work locally. This place kept a team of Suffolk craftsmen going for a year.'

'Right. But you've finished here now, I take it? Hope you have. Well, shall we mingle with the crowd? I see some faces even I recognise. Let's just hope they don't recognise me. Cast a discreet glance, will you, at the blokes over there at the table under the apple tree. I've got mug shots of the lot of them back at HQ. And one of them has just got back from Spain. The tall one with the full suntan. Flew in from the Costa del Crime two days ago. Stay well away from *him,* Ellie.' He fell silent for a moment, glancing around uneasily, eyes seeking the gesticulating figure of their host and flicking back to the visitor from Spain. 'This could turn nasty. I wonder if old Ron's aware of the serpent lurking in his shrubbery?' he murmured. 'I do hope he's slipped on his steel-lined Y-fronts. He's annoyed some influential people lately. Could have brought down a painful retribution on his head. Or other more sensitive parts of his anatomy.'

'Those blokes don't look at all suspicious to me. Just like the other men here—successful businessmen, you'd say. They probably give generously to charity and own half a race-horse.'

'And support a heavy alimony habit,' said Jennings, 'judging by the third wives clustering around.'

'How can you tell they're third wives?'

'Not difficult. Get your eye in, Ellie. First wives at this binge are in gold lamé and real jewels, dressed for a night at the Royal Opera House . . . a night twenty years ago. The second wives are in Chloë and Manolos with a spray tan, streaked hair and a watchful expression. Third wives are young and skinny as alley-cats and tug at their hair extensions in boredom. They'd rather be back home watching the *X Factor*.'

I looked at him in surprise. It occurred to me that I really knew very little about DI Jennings. 'I had no idea you were so observant! What are you then? Some sort of profiler? Okay, Mr. Clever, tell me what category Alicia comes into.'

He pretended to reflect. '"Not immediately obvious. Dark-hair and mysterious dark eyes. Intelligent looking. Far too good for Ron. Stylish woman. Chanel, would you say—that white clinging thing? Something as tasteful as it's expensive, anyway. She's a good bit younger than Ron so I'll go for second wife but with more than a touch of independence about her.'

'You're pretty good. That's right. Except I know she favours Dior. Not sure I'd know the difference. Second wife, ambitious, wealthy in her own right. Family money—that's what gives her the independence you've noticed. You know—I've actually heard some women say—squirming with gratitude: "He's offered to give me a new kitchen!" I pass those jobs straight on to Charles. Now, Alicia tells Ron what he's going to get! And she has the sense to listen to the experts she's paying. But all this is rather alarming. Lord knows what pigeon-hole you've put *me* into.'

His face softened. 'Can't categorise you. A one off. Nearest I can get is arty-chic. In that floating greenery-yellery thing you've got on, you'd better watch out. Wander off into the orchard in the gloaming and the Spirits of the Place will claim you for their own. I don't want to have to explain you've been carried off by a hairy-legged woodland faun to the sound of pan-pipes. So stay close to me.'

I shivered and decided that would be no problem.

*   *   *

We ate supper at a table with people I knew in the rose-draped marquee. We danced and chatted, but I waited in vain for Richard to suggest a stroll through the orchard or the herb garden. Annoyingly, he seemed happy to stay in the candle-lit orbit of the other guests, drinking sparingly, eyes watchful.

After darkness had fallen he suddenly checked the time, excused himself and set off in the direction of the cloakrooms. He returned quickly and smiling said: 'Ellie, before it gets too late, why don't you do as our host invited and show me round your handiwork? The house seems to be open—there are people wandering in and out.'

Puzzled, I accompanied him as he walked quickly from room to room on the ground floor even poking his nose into the outside log store and the gardener's lavatory.

'Not thinking of making an offer for it, are you, Richard?'

'I only wish! Upstairs? Did you have a hand in that?'

'Not really. I just oversaw the refurbishment and reconstruction of the original fittings. Cosmetic mostly. Still it's pretty glamorous up there. Alicia's had the good taste to leave

115

well alone and let the bones of the house show through. You can get a real feel for medieval living. Of course, it's a wonderful foil for *her* with her *belle dame sans merci* looks. You know—all that lily on the brow, and on thy cheeks a fading rose . . .'

'I think that was her love-lorne knight-at-arms?' he corrected. 'The lady herself was:

'Full   beautiful—a   faery's   child,'   he murmured, trotting upstairs ahead of me.

Her hair was long, her foot was light,
And her eyes were wild.'

'Mmm . . . yes . . . I can just see the Lady Alicia sighing and moaning in these surroundings. Not so sure about old Ron,' he said shining a slim torch onto ancient timbers, tapestries, copper bowls of pot-pourri and coarse rush carpets underfoot. A swift inspection of the rooms revealed draped four-poster beds, two of them suspiciously a-tremble.

Finally, 'Is there any room we haven't looked into?' he asked.

'Only the space Ron mentioned—the Priest's Hole. This was a Roman Catholic house in a sea of Parliamentary supporters. They had to have somewhere to hide the visiting clergy from Cromwell's squaddies.'

'Show me.'

The narrow space was cleverly contrived between two rooms in such a way that the regular march of the windows was not interrupted. I showed him the exact spot to press on the panelling which sprang back an inch, allowing me to put my fingers behind it and slide it back sideways, revealing a closed door.

As I clicked on the external light, I had sudden misgivings. 'I don't feel comfortable doing this,' I said. 'Well you never know what we might disturb . . . There's a sort of day bed in there . . . Champagne flowing for hours . . . Some people might think it the perfect spot for a bit of . . .'

He wasn't listening. 'Tell me what this stuff is,' he said, shining the torch onto the carpet. 'These bits of loose vegetable matter.'

'Um. Oh, that'll be dried hops.'

'Hops? What are you on about?'

'This was once the house of a Suffolk brewing family. I found bits of equipment about the place, even traces of hops they used as ingredients in the beer making stashed away in the rafters. Alicia thought it was very romantic. She had some fresh hop garlands sent from Hereford and draped them all over the beams in there. She thought it made the place smell herby. She was right, actually. But I see what you're getting at,' I said, lowering my voice. 'Someone's been in here. Let's go away.'

But he had already thrown the door open. I peered over his outstretched arm as he stood, shocked and silent, taking in the scene. 'Oh my God!' he breathed. 'Oh, how could we have got it so wrong?'

*   *   *

I wriggled under his arm and stood, wide-eyed and staring.

As I had feared, the room was occupied.

A figure, apparently asleep, was draped elegantly over the day-bed. Alicia was unnaturally still. Her silk dress flowed along, outlining her slender limbs; one high-heeled diamanté sandal hung negligently from her toe, the other lay discarded by the bed. Her black hair snaked across the pillow outlining her pallid features. Around her neck was knotted with crazy insouciance a man's black bow tie. On a small table at her elbow were two glasses of pink champagne still fizzing energetically with life, an obscene note in what I was quite certain was a place of death.

Jennings sprang into action, pushing me into a corner and performing the automatic gestures to check for signs of life. He shook his head. 'She's dead,' he said. 'And only minutes ago, I'd say.' He took his cell phone from his pocket and made two crisp calls, unintelligible to me.

'But why is she dead?' I squeaked. 'What happened? Heart attack? There's no blood.'

Jennings delicately eased the bow tie away from the throat with his fingers. 'Mustn't ruin the scene for SOCO,' he commented.

'Shouldn't be doing this but I have to know . . . Ah, now there's a touch Dior never thought of. She's been throttled with this and then some joker re-tied it in the approved manner. Some cool nerve! Takes me forever to knot my own and here's someone meticulously tying it around the neck of a woman he's just squeezed the life out of. The killer leaving his calling card?'

I began to shake with horror as the enormity of the scene hit me. 'That's mad! It's sick! It's . . . it's . . . so calculated . . . passionless! Who would . . .?'

'Ally! Alicia! You up here? The Tennisons are just leaving and would like to say goodbye. I say—Ally!'

Heavy feet thumped along the corridor and doors banged open and shut. Jennings stepped into the corridor. 'In here Redmayne!' he said.

*　　　*　　　*

In the end, I had to admit Ron had behaved rather well. Demands for instant police assistance had been cut short by the quick flash of a warrant card, a short explanation, one or two more phone calls. Jennings was in charge and wheels unnoticed by anyone were in motion. With a second shock that evening, I realised that my invitation had been attractive to the inspector not so much for the pleasure of my company as for the innocent entrée it

119

had provided for the county's top brass into a scene the police wished to observe more closely.

Ron was pointing to the tie at his wife's neck. 'Well there you are, Mr. Plod,' he said to Jennings. 'Even I could solve this one. Line the male guests up against the stable wall, target the one without a necktie and shoot 'im. Easy peasy. And anyway,' he said with the trace of a smug leer, 'I recognise this one. Huh! Silk with silver stripes! It's a bit fancy and wouldn't it be! I can lead you straight to its fancy owner. The Cambridge Casanova!' He stared for a moment at the pair of champagne glasses. 'Cheating cow!' was his epitaph on his dead wife.

The uniformed support was already in place below and again I wondered at the speed of deployment. Female guests were being ushered into the drawing room of the house but I managed to stay close to Jennings, pretending to assist. The men were herded into the marquee. One or two were being sent back, grumbling, from the car park.

It could have been laughable. I had to swallow back giggles of hysteria as I surveyed the line up of fifty puzzled and outraged guests. Forty-nine were still more or less correctly attired. Only one sported a shirt open at the neck. Tall and good-looking with a boyish shock of yellow hair and merry blue eyes, he was familiar to me. 'Marcus de

Staines,' I whispered to Jennings. 'The chinless and now apparently tie-less wonder. Heart-throb of day-time tv. Medieval historian of repute.'

'Well, let's see what this will do for his reputation,' said Jennings. With a cold gesture he attempted to calm Ron who was twitching with vindictive glee and pointing the righteous finger of an outraged husband at the young man.

'That's him! That's the bastard who's murdered Alicia!' Ron broke out. 'No tie! Look—no tie! That's the . . .' he dredged his vocabulary for a suitably medieval epithet, '. . . cuckolding killer! He should be stocked, pilloried, hung, drawn and quartered!'

Jennings set about rescuing the astonished and red-faced don from the hideous scene which seemed about to break out. With the relief of men who suddenly find the cloud of suspicion has lifted from them, they were responding in varying degrees of outrage, turning, predictably, on the guilty party. 'I say! Good Lord! What an arsehole! Can't believe it!' Fists were clenched. The Lord High Sheriff of Essex called for order. A retired Lieutenant-Colonel reached for a phantom sabre at his side. Warrant card flashing, Jennings moved through them, confident and calming.

'Just step this way with me, sir,' he said mildly, cutting de Staines out of the crowd. 'A few things to clear up if you wouldn't mind.'

I found I'd been left behind with Ron. A minute later we'd retreated to the kitchen and I was going through the familiar ritual of making him a cup of tea. Earl Grey, two lumps. To my alarm, as the shock and tension cleared he grabbed me and sobbed noisily into my shoulder. 'I'm such a fool, Ellie! How can I not have seen what was going on? Had you any idea?' He looked up at me with a sudden shaft of suspicion. 'The pair of you were pretty thick, I always thought . . . Did she never . . .? No?' He sniffed and gulped and I offered him a sheet of kitchen paper. 'All those working historical weekends away! And they were at it under my roof! In my own Priest's Hole!'

He recovered sufficiently to take a comforting sip of tea. 'Tell your boyfriend thank you from me, will you Ellie? For being here. Taking control. Piece of luck a policeman being right there on the spot! And a smart one at that. I mean—what are the chances of a Cambridge criminologist tripping over the body? That would really have appealed to Alicia.' He sighed with respect for the artistic sensitivity of his dead wife then, quickly changing emotional gear, his eyes narrowed in sudden thought and he confided: 'Sorry to say such a thing at such a time . . . probably very inappropriate but . . . this could do his career no harm, you know. Your young man, I mean. Had you thought of that?'

'No, Ron,' I said through gritted teeth. 'But I'm sure *he* has.'

* * *

I finally caught up with my escort in the car park. It had been transformed into a crime scene. Blue and white plastic ribbons fluttered, outlining the field, arc lamps illuminated with a ghastly glow the guests, silent now and shell-shocked, who were being ushered back into the real world by the two valets, now openly wearing their police id's.

A police car eased up and I watched as Marcus de Staines was handed into the back seat and driven off. A second car drove over to Jennings and he opened the rear door. He gestured to a group of officers and they came forward leading a figure I recognised from the party. Now in plastic handcuffs and—oddly—without his shoes—he trod gingerly in his socks through the rutted stubble to the car and with a brief sneer for Jennings, slid inside.

Two minutes later the same procedure was repeated as Ron emerged from the house, being hustled along between two officers.

'*Three* suspects, Richard? Marcus, Ron and Sun-Tan-Man? That's quite a haul for one night. Are there any more? Would you mind telling me what's going on?' I said.

'Sorry. Not the time. Not the place,' he said. 'But I'll tell you what is. Ten minutes from now. Your cottage. I can leave all this to the scene of crime officers now and my sergeant. Shall we make a run for it?'

I realised that he was on the point of exhaustion and gently prised his car keys from his hand.

*   *   *

'Blue Mountain be all right?' I called from the kitchen.

'Rather have cocoa,' came the sleepy reply.

I settled with my drink on a cushion at his feet as he slumped on her sofa. 'Poor young man! Poor silly Marcus!' I said. 'Why do you suppose he did it? I expect she'd refused to run away with him. Led him on and then decided at the last minute to stick with her husband.'

'Not at all,' he said. 'She was well up for it. They were going away together. Tickets booked for Istanbul next Tuesday.'

'Oh, no! And Ron found out, followed them upstairs, found them in flagrante delicto and killed her?'

'First saying: Would you mind removing your tie, old man, just the thing I need to strangle this strumpet? Come on, Ellie! I'll give you a clue—neither Marcus nor Ron went near that room before she died.'

I thought for a minute. 'The hops? That bloke you were marching through the car park in his socks?'

124

'Yes. The leathery mystery man from Spain. I had his shoes bagged. He'd got traces of hops on the soles. He was up there all right.'

'Wow! Was *he* Alicia's lover too?'

'No. Her killer. A hired killer. It's what he does.'

'But he didn't look like a . . . what would you call him? A hit man!' I protested, trying and failing to recollect his features.

'What would you expect? A pony tail, tattoos and dirty finger-nails? Nah! They blend in. He was just a man in an evening suit like all the others. Ex-army officer gone wrong. Well-educated, man of the world. But with a taste for killing and cash. I thought I was watching him pretty closely but I must have stared a second too long into your eyes and there he was—or rather—wasn't.'

'And I hardly need to ask whose signature was on his pay cheque?'

'Ron's! We got it so wrong Ellie! We've been keeping an eye on Ron and his shady dealings for some time and when another of our familiar faces cut loose from his sunny retreat and embarked on a jaunt to deepest Suffolk we assumed Ron himself was the target. Plenty of people would have been grateful for that! But there I was, all prepared to defend our host against evil-doers. When I noticed Sun Tan Man had gone missing from the party I rang my lads in the car park and told them to hang on to him if he fetched up there. Just in case. As they were holding his keys—no problem. I dashed through the house expecting to find our host bludgeoned to death in the billiard room . . . garrotted in the garage . . . but no—it was our newly ennobled lord himself who was doing the hiring.'

'Because Alicia had been disporting herself with a don? Hardly makes sense, Richard. I mean, I know—knew—them as a couple—he'd have smacked her across the chops and threatened to horsewhip the guy. She'd have responded by beating him to a pulp and walking out. At the very worst he'd have sold his story to a red-top news-sheet. He wouldn't even have bothered to divorce her—not with alimony being what it is these days.'

'Exactly! You're getting there! Follow the money! He was about to lose a fortune whichever way you look at it. Her own wealth would no longer be available to him and he might well find himself caught in the steel jaws of alimony payments. And then there's the not-negligible sum she'd settled on him in insurance. They had reciprocal policies. A lot at risk, Ellie.'

'So, enter the killer. But what was all that business with the tie, Richard?'

'The killing was staged-managed by Ron but only to an extent, I think. He knew of his wife's assignation: the killer moved off straight after her when she went upstairs, beating her lover to it. I interviewed the luckless don

126

and he told me he was buttonholed by Ron and a couple of his mates who held him in conversation. It rather put him off his stroke and he didn't dare shoot straight off upstairs. Ron knew that you can't just have the body of your wife discovered in your house without raising suspicions and bringing a nuisance of a police officer or two onto the scene. He was watching out for someone who could witness the discovery of the body. Any of the guests cornered and given the tour of the house would have filled the bill.'

'And we, respectable souls that we are, fitted nicely.'

'That's right. Then, distraught with grief—well as near as Ron could manage—he was able to identify the neck tie and direct attention to the poor sap he'd set up to take the blame. The tie was a nice touch. It could have been a credit card, a cell phone, a sheet of runic script, anything of de Staines's to put him at the scene. Taking revenge on the man who'd deceived him into the bargain. Neat.'

'De Staines told me he'd taken his tie off along with his jacket in the gents to wash his face and cool off when he got back from piggling about in the roof—and freshening himself up for his tryst with Alicia no doubt. When he'd got the soap out of his eyes and looked up the tie had disappeared. Several blokes had gone into the gents at the same time and left in a bunch. He couldn't say who'd taken it. A silly prank, he thought or a genuine mistake. That little touch would have been the killer's own. Opportunistic. No way he could have planned it. They like to improvise at the scene—use what's to hand.'

'But why re-tie it so perfectly?'

'Our man goes in for the whimsical touch. It's his signature. Gets him a rep in the right quarters—the artist of assassination.'

'Ghastly, murdering old Ron! To think I made him a cup of tea! Let him slobber all over my Missoni frock! What'll happen to him now?'

The inspector grinned with satisfaction. 'At this moment, Ron's in an office at HQ in front of a flickering screen commenting on his financial affairs to an interested team of specialists. No telling how high his dubious connections go, but it's high! We've been longing to make our way through to that.'

'Ah. Well. Glad I was able to be of some help,' I said stonily. 'Here's hoping I've inadvertently brought down the government. Some good at least will have come of it.'

He took my cup from me and placed it with his on a table. In a second he'd slid to the floor and clamped me in a tight hug. 'Sorry about that. Unforgivable! Because I was preoccupied it doesn't mean I wasn't having a good time! All the same—not quite my scene. This is more like it.

'I say, Ellie,' he said uncertainly, tugging at

128

his throat, 'you won't misinterpret the gesture
. . . won't scream blue murder and run a mile,
will you, if I start to take off this bloody awful
tie?'

DIE LIKE A MAHARAJAH

An Ellie Hardwick, Architect, Mystery.

'Why don't you ask little Miss Know-It-All? She's over there by the lake pretending to sketch. I bet *she* can identify it for you. *And* give you the Latin name for it into the bargain! . . . Oh, you're all such *weeds*! *I'll* go and find out.'

The penetrating voice of Phyllis Wickham-Skeith carried clearly as far as my ears through the still air of an Indian afternoon. She probably hadn't intended me to overhear, I decided generously. I didn't look up. I felt rather than heard the embarrassed murmuring from the rest of the group as they turned and walked away and, a moment later: 'Ah, there you are, Ellie dear! Now do tell—we're all dying to know—exactly what is this pretty little flower? We were all sure you'd be able to identify it. We would have asked our guide . . .' She looked about her theatrically, 'but Govind always seems to be indulging in some religious observance when one wants to consult him.'

'Sensible bloke, Govind,' I thought bitterly. 'Now, why don't we all adopt a mysterious oriental religion which compels our absence for a few minutes when Phyllis is on the prowl with her incessant and mindless questions?'

I took the silky pink lotus bud she was flourishing and put on a show of interest.

'Ah, yes. This is undoubtedly *Jalebi Pavarti*.' Between clenched teeth I muttered something which could be taken for Hindi—by someone who didn't speak Hindi. It was an item I remembered from last night's menu.

'There! I thought you'd know! Now, how do you say that in English?'

'*Pavarti's Nipple*,' I said, improvising and praying the Hindu goddess of Love wouldn't strike me down for my disrespect.

Prudish Phyllis wouldn't rush to broadcast that piece of information! Predictably, she lost all interest in the lotus and dropped it, unregarded now, on the grass. But she hadn't finished with me yet. She approached the painting I was busy with and peered over my shoulder. I cringed and tried to block her view in that protective gesture that comes automatically to third-rate painters like me.

There was nothing third-rate about the subject, though. It was a scene worth painting. Peacocks strutted across lush lawns which swept in a very English way up to the elegant façade of the hunting lodge of the Maharajas of Ulmar. Of palatial size, the lodge was a blend of eastern and western architectural styles as perceived by one of the cleverest architects of his day. Sir James Hardwick had combined practicality and pomp with wit and genius to produce in 1880 the essential must-have for the Maharajahs of Rajputana. It had been widely admired and Sir James had found himself much in demand all over India. Even the great Sir Edwin Lutyens had been influenced by his style.

'Good one, great-great-grandfather!' I thought, with a rush of pride in my ancestor and I flicked a highlight on the glowing amber stones I'd tried to reproduce on my watercolour. 'Glad I came and saw your stuff for myself!' I intended to work the picture up when I got home to Suffolk and hang it on the office wall.

'Why don't you just take a photograph, Ellie?' came the querulous voice of Phyllis over my shoulder. 'The camera gives a much more reliable record I always say. And, anyway, you won't have time to finish that— we're due back on the coach in half an hour. They're loading our suitcases already.'

I flicked a bit more and pretended not to hear her.

'You really ought to put in a scale figure, you know, otherwise it could be taken for a dolls' house—or something the size of Blenheim. And you could, with advantage, miss out half those curlicues. There—below the pediment . . . Too much of a flourish— don't you agree? Far too complex. These Indian architects just don't know when to leave well alone!'

'Thank you Phyllis,' I said truculently. I

132

looked at my watch. 'Oh, dear! You're right. I *am* short of time. You wouldn't just pop down to the lake and gather up a fully-blown sample of one of those Pavarti Specials would you? I noticed a whole colony of them at the lake's edge by that little pavilion. I'd like to take a closer look at one . . . perhaps make a quick sketch . . . identify it properly,' I said. 'And while you're down there why don't you just jump in and swim with the crocodiles?' I added but I didn't say it aloud.

Anyone else would have known I was just trying to get rid of her but another of Phyllis's traits was that she loved to be seen to be of use. She hurried off towards the lake and I was left in peace. The tour group was a small one— thirteen—and I was the unlucky thirteenth. The others were comfortably in couples and I was uncomfortably by myself. I would have been even less at ease, however, had the fourteenth member of the party turned up as scheduled. An on and off relationship had clicked into reverse gear a fortnight before the holiday and one of us had to cancel. Without too much heartache, Jack had elected to go off to the Caribbean with my cousin. I had thought the tour would rid me of my seething anger but there are some conditions not even the colour and splendour of India can cure.

We were touring Rajasthan staying in ancient royal palaces, decorated merchants' houses or, as today, in country houses complete with game reserves and waterholes for wild life. This was the last day of the 'Live Like a Maharajah' tour and we were setting off very shortly for Delhi and the jet back to Heathrow. I had grown to like my fellow travellers. They were an ill-assorted bunch but we all had one thing in common—we all hated Phyllis. And I include in this club her husband, Timothy.

It wouldn't be fair to say he was *hen*-pecked. Have you ever seen a goose go on the attack? Forward rush, wings flapping, beak open? That was more Phyllis's style. And the years of stepping out of her way had taken their toll. Timothy was middle-aged with greying fair hair, pale blue eyes and that long sheep's face that some English academics have. He looked like something that had been forced to grow in a cellar. I think he was probably quite attractive when he was young. Before he met Phyllis. But now he was hesitant, uncommunicative, a man cringing inside a shell he'd built for himself.

We tried to cheer him up and anaesthetise the wounds made by Phyllis's barbed remarks. With a laugh or a complicitous smile we tried to convey to Timothy that we understood. It was OK. He wasn't to concern himself if his wife had the sensitivity of an armoured tank and a voice that could shatter glass. The brunt of all this reassurance fell on kind-hearted Paula Parrish from Godalming who had appointed herself chairman of the T.W-S Protection Society and encouraged the rest of us to distract Phyllis's attention from him whenever we could.

'Give the poor old thing a break,' she'd said on Day 4 (Jewels of Jaipur). 'He's ever so interesting when you get him on his own. He's a historian, did you know that? And a very well-known one! He writes books on the Moghul Empire and that's why they've come on this tour. He's following in the tracks of the Emperor Akhbar, apparently. Now that would make a good TV programme, don't you think?'

'Shove over Simon Schama!' laughed her partner Ben, a dentist Paula had confided she was 'trying out'.

'You'd think Phyllis would take more of an interest, wouldn't you? Push him along a bit instead of always putting him down. What's her problem?' Paula wondered.

By Day 5 (Marvels Of Mewar) Caroline Hughes thought she had the answer. 'She just doesn't like men! You should hear what she said to my husband at breakfast yesterday. Tell them, Steve!'

Steve demurred.

'Don't worry about it, mate,' said Ben cheerily. 'She's done it to all the blokes! Tongue like a scalpel! Snip! Snip! Just remember not to touch the meatballs vindaloo.'

135

'It's poor old Govind I feel sorry for,' said Liz Cresswell, taking up the tale. 'Do you know she's threatened to report him to the tour firm? I heard her taking his name and number . . . said he'd been . . . what was it, Larry?'

'Neglectful . . . inattentive . . . incompetent . . . something like that.'

'Can you swear to that?' The clipped tones of Colonel Richard Thwaite (British Army Retired) sounded like the cocking of a rifle.

Larry straightened and replied smartly, 'Those were the repeatable epithets. She's going to lodge a formal complaint with "Tracks East" when we get back to London.'

Colonel Thwaite considered this. 'Indeed?' he said. 'Govind has a young family, I understand. This job's important to him and it seems to me that a chap's career should not be put on the line at the whim of this lady whose judgement I would have considered questionable.' He raked the group with a narrow-eyed blue glare. 'Do you agree?'

We agreed. We'd have agreed to follow Colonel Thwaite over the top. Any top.

'Govind's wonderful!' Everyone hurried to present their own account of the Hindu guide's humorous and deeply knowledgeable contribution to the holiday.

But now it was Day 14 (Dreams of the Desert) and it was drawing to a close. A welcome close for everyone. The trip had been too long by a few days and a few hundred miles, too hot, too mesmerising and too full of Phyllis. All eyes and minds were on transport: the coach to Delhi where we would have a last supper and the BA jet we would catch in the early hours of the morning.

In a spirit of defiance I stayed at my easel after Phyllis walked off and worked on my painting for a further twenty minutes. Nothing more interrupted my solitary pleasure. I enjoyed the hot, earthy smells, the distant fluting laughter of the flock of girls in bright saris of acid yellow, pink and jade green who wandered elegantly about the gardens, baskets on heads, pruning and tidying the already immaculate grounds. Behind me a troop of langur monkeys quarrelled noisily in a tree top and a peacock gave an ear-splitting shriek.

I left the painting under the tree to dry off. It wouldn't take long in this heat. In the meantime I made my way over to the coach where the others were beginning to gather. In the efficient Indian way, all was ready a good half hour before the estimated time of departure and the group was assembling, water bottles in hand, sun hats on. Govind had trained us well.

The last few stragglers strolled in from the lake and the palace and the count began. Unusually, Govind was not in attendance and the bus-driver who knew us all by now and was learning his numbers in English began to count heads.

'Twelve guests,' he announced. 'Twelve.' He held up one finger.

'Come in now number thirteen,' said a chirpy male voice. 'Your time's up!'

'Phyllis?' said another voice uncertainly. 'I say—anyone seen Phyllis? Ah, here comes Govind. Govind, my wife appears to be missing!'

*   *   *

The body was retrieved from the centre of the lake by the hotel wild-life warden who had taken a boat out on sighting something white bobbing on the surface.

*   *   *

'It's my fault she's dead!' I wailed again. 'If I hadn't sent her to pick a lotus bud . . .'

The other ten made comforting noises and Paula passed me a pack of tissues. We were all strained and agitated. We were herded together in the sumptuous surroundings of the Polo Bar but the red plush, the gold and mahogany did little to lift our spirits. The men anxiously checked their watches every five minutes.

'Do you think they'll keep us much longer?' said Steve. 'I've got a conference on Thursday. Can't afford to miss that plane! How much longer do you suppose they'll grill him for?

They've had him in there for ages.'

'Well, when a wife dies in India I expect the first thing you do is check out the husband,' said Bill, a retired barrister. '*I* would. They can hardly suspect poor old Tim of bumping her off for her dowry though! If ever there was one, it would be long gone, I should imagine. Anyway—relax! I think the investigation's in good hands. That was a very impressive young man. What was his name? Hari Singh—yes, that was it.'

The tall, rangy Inspector of the Rajasthan Police CID had been quite a surprise. He and his sergeant had drawn up in a white Landrover emblazoned with the motto of the force in Hindi and English. We all noted that they were 'Committed To Serve'. We were further reassured by his professional manner and his efficiency and by the fact that he spoke better English than most of the group. But his gaze had gone through us like a lance as he lined us up for a briefing and the smart khaki uniform, I recognised, was a thin disguise for the Rajput warrior underneath. He had stated his intention of interviewing each of us and had begun by isolating and then questioning Timothy Wickham-Skeith.

'Come off it, Bill!' Steve protested. 'It was plainly an accident. Misadventure . . . whatever you like. Happens all the time. I think the hotel is much to be blamed for not posting danger notices.'

'What? And put off the tourists?' said Bill. *'BEWARE CROCODILES*—that's going to look good in the foreground of everyone's holiday snaps, isn't it? And, be fair, now— they did warn us about them. But remember this area's suffering from a vast reduction in tourism at the moment. They can't afford for any more visitors to be put off by a shock-horror story like this finding its way onto the internet or page one of the tabloids.' He narrowed his eyes, and swept us all with a barrister's air of secret knowledge. 'Hmm . . . we might find that useful. And the fact that there's been such a hoo-ha over the next test match series. It's due to take place next month in Delhi. Lots of visitors expected. Boost to the economy. India will beat us hollow, of course, and they're looking forward to that.'

'But the English team's playing silly buggers . . . threatening a boycott,' said Steve, catching on. 'It wouldn't take much to turn this into a double media disaster. See what you're getting at, Bill. They'll want to avoid any adverse publicity. Can't afford another fiasco like the Greek one last year . . . Did those blokes ever get back home? Stands to reason. Nothing if not diplomatic, Indians. They'll do the right thing. We'll all be shipped out on the next plane—out of their hair!'

'Quite agree!' said Colonel Thwaite. 'That would be their best plan. Swift, sensible, discreet. The last thing they want is news coverage of some dotty lotus-gathering memsahib getting herself gobbled up by a crocodile. We'll get our marching orders any minute.'

But an hour later, Timothy was still closeted with the Inspector.

'What if—heaven forbid!—they were to accuse poor Timothy of murder? What would they do with him?' asked Paula in distress.

'Arrest him. Hold him. Try him eventually,' said Bill. 'And we all noticed the local lock-up.'

Several shivered at the memory of the desolate concrete block of a prison we had driven past the previous day.

'We can't let that happen! Can we?' said Paula. 'We can't leave him behind in a place like that to struggle with a foreign justice system! Come on—we've got to get together on this!'

'Quite right, Mrs. Parrish,' said the Colonel. 'And I think it's clear what our tactics must be.' He smiled a thin smile. 'Their first error was to leave us all together in the same room.'

Through my grief and shock and self-recrimination an idea had been bubbling. 'Look,' I said, 'you don't have to worry about making up a story. If it comes down to giving an alibi, we don't need to dream anything up. I can *prove* that Timothy had nothing to do with his wife's death. But let's not force the Inspector's hand. I'll just go in when my turn comes—he said he'd take us in alphabetical order.' I looked around. 'So that puts just the two Cresswells ahead of me.'

The two Cresswells were duly called and were finished in ten minutes. I took a deep breath on hearing my name announced and strode as confidently as I could on knocking knees into the presence of Inspector Hari Singh and his sergeant. The inspector was seated behind the gleaming expanse of the manager's desk, the office and IT equipment commandeered by the Rajasthan Police.

'And you, I suspect, are Miss Hardwick?' The voice was deep and smooth but with an edge of grittiness.

I confirmed his suspicions. He waved a negligent hand at a bronze bust which sat in the centre of the mantelpiece. 'The same name as the honourable architect of this magnificent pile.'

'The same family,' I admitted. 'The same profession, though I'm still working at the reputation.'

He grinned and asked a few basic questions. His sergeant tapped away at the keyboard of his lap-top. He studied the screen and gave a confirmatory nod to the inspector. Hari Singh noticed my wondering glance and unbent a little. 'Sergeant Mishra has a degree from the London School of Economics,' he commented. He waited for my admiring murmur and pursued his theme. 'The Rajasthan Police do not spend their time hurrying to the scene of dacoity and dowry crimes on a camel as some westerners imagine. You are most likely these days to find us hacking our way through the thickets of the cyber-crime jungle. Death by crocodile has a very old-fashioned ring to it.'

'She did die . . . um . . . by crocodile, then?' I asked, mortified. 'We didn't know for certain. No one's told us anything.'

'The remains are at present undergoing a post-mortem examination at the Medical College Hospital but a preliminary inspection by our police doctor indicates that death was caused by loss of blood, shock and possibly drowning following the severance of limbs.'

'Drowning?'

'Yes. It's possible,' he said. 'Even likely. This is not the first death by crocodile the lake has witnessed. In the nineteenth century the Maharajah of the day, a keen sportsman, was duck-shooting from a gilded punt in the centre of the lake. The explosive shotgun device he had had fixed to the prow backfired and hurled the unfortunate prince into the water. Witnesses report that His Highness was carried twice around the lake by one of these creatures, screaming, until he finally died—of drowning.'

'So Phyllis's death has a royal precedent,' I burbled. 'She'd have been pleased . . .' Was he deliberately trying to shock me? Of course he was.

'I am eager, as you might imagine,

143

to establish how the lady came to put herself within range of a three metre long crocodile. So, perhaps you can help me to fill in the background? We calculate that the unfortunate demise occurred at around one thirty so if you could account for your movements, let's say, between one and two?'

I told him about my conversation with Phyllis, admitting it was at my suggestion that she had gone to pick a lotus flower. Tears ran down my face and I was glad of Paula's stash of Kleenex. I told him about the peacock cry I had heard which, with hindsight, could have been Phyllis's scream of surprise and horror.

'You were not aware that it is from that place by the pavilion that the crocodiles are fed by the Forest Rangers?' he asked bluntly. 'Chickens, pigs and goats are their usual food.'

'No, I didn't know,' I whispered. I was devastated. And I didn't like the way the questioning was going. I rallied. 'Look, Inspector, the dietary regimen of the estate wild life and the domestic arrangements of the hotel management have not been explained to us. It was doubtless considered less than interesting.'

He glared at me and I thought I might have gone too far. 'Don't challenge!' I told myself and cried some more.

And now came the question I had been waiting for.

'Did you see anyone else in the vicinity

while you were painting?'

I sniffed and wrinkled my brow in concern. 'You're not suggesting someone was involved in her death?' I asked, horrified.

He sighed. 'You go unerringly to the heart of our enquiry, Miss Hardwick. Did she fall or was she pushed? That is exactly what I am trying to ascertain. Now, if you would answer my question?'

'Well, there were lots of people milling around by the coach but I only had one person in focus the whole time,' I said thoughtfully. 'Timothy. Mr. Wickam-Skeith.'

The lance gaze pinned me to my seat but I squeezed my knees together and stared innocently back.

'He was sitting under the acacia tree between me and the palace about a hundred yards from the lake. He was reading a book. He arrived at . . . oh . . . just after one—we'd all had an early lunch—and got up to go back to the coach just before I packed up at one forty. Is this important? Look, I can show you exactly what was happening at the time of death if that's what you want to establish!' I said, allowing a thread of excitement to creep into my voice.

I heaved my big leather hold-all onto my knee and made a show of searching around in the depths, failing to find what I was looking for. My hand encountered the small sleek shape of my camera and I thrust it deeper into the bag. 'Drat! I left it to dry under the tree. My watercolour. In all the excitement I forgot about it. Do you think someone could fetch it?'

A nod to the sergeant sent him scurrying off and Hari Singh and I spent an uncomfortable six and a half minutes discussing Indo-Sarassenic architecture and the incompetence of English bowlers.

The sergeant had obviously taken time to look at my painting himself as he presented it with a smile and a flourish. The inspector studied it, even scratched at the paint with a manicured finger-nail. I waited patiently. I watched him take in every detail of the peaceful scene: the palace in the background, the arching stable gate, so English with its blue-faced clock, the fingers frozen on one thirty; the bucolic figure of Timothy, looking suitably Victorian, I thought, straw hat on head and book in lap, lounging under the acacia tree. My scale figure. Hurriedly painted in at Phyllis's suggestion.

'May I keep this for my files?' asked the inspector.

I smiled and nodded and began to gather up my things. I thought I'd better not offer to sign it.

*   *   *

I was never quite sure whose relief had been

the greater—the tourists' or that of the Rajasthan Police as we set off for Delhi and the airport. We all climbed aboard the BA jet in the early hours of the following morning. Not quite all. Timothy had stayed behind with the 'Tracks East' representative to help organise the funeral. Oddly, we thought, he was not having the body shipped back home but was intending to have her cremated and her ashes scattered in the river in the Hindu custom. Paula and her partner gallantly offered to stay behind at the expense of the tour operator to keep him company.

*   *   *

It was a month before I screwed up the courage to unpack my camera. I didn't want to know. I'd taken my old-fashioned but reliable Leica with me—the kind that still used film. When I collected the developed prints, I finally settled down to examine them. I found myself feverishly flipping through the images of gilded palaces and domes, caparisoned elephants, heavily-laden camel trains, crowds of laughing girls with copper milk pots on their heads. I was looking for Day 14. And there it was, bringing back the sunny clarity of that last golden afternoon. The stable clock stood at twenty minutes past one, the peacocks strutted on shaven lawns, the lotus-fringed lake sparkled enticingly and in the shade of the acacia tree there lounged Timothy Wickham-Skeith.

I was limp with relief. I had been ready to destroy the evidence of my lie—if it *was* a lie—to the police. During our detention in the Polo Bar, I had been totally unable to remember whether Timothy had been under the tree. I remembered painting him in, goaded by Phyllis's waspish comment about scale, but I couldn't have stood in a court of law and sworn that he had been there at the crucial time. I could have produced my photographs for the inspector there and then but I wasn't confident enough to gamble a man's liberty on what would be revealed. But my instinct had been right all along and I was glad to have the evidence of his innocence.

'Why don't you just take a photo, Ellie?' Phyllis had said.

I had taken her advice.

In fact, I'd taken three photos. It helps to have a panorama when I'm recording architectural scenes. I turned to the remaining shots. The right of the trio of pictures showed a gang of langurs gambolling at the foot of a cedar tree and the wing of the hunting lodge in the background. The left showed the lake's edge and the west wing. On the carriage sweep stood the coach with remembered figures clustering about it. And there was another figure on the lakeside path determinedly making its way southwards, one arm raised in

148

greeting. The green silk shirt looked familiar to me. I got out my magnifying glass and checked. I was not mistaken. It occurred to me that this person might have sighted Phyllis for if Phyllis had been behind me moving west towards the lake edge simultaneously—and she was—I calculated that these two figures would have met up with each other exactly at the pavilion where Phyllis had fallen foul of the crocodile.

I looked and looked again at the innocent-seeming scenario. And, of course, at the moment the camera had recorded its evidence, no crime had been committed. No accident had occurred. The meeting could have been innocent and unplanned. What could have happened in ten minutes? What actions or words had resulted in a hideous death so shortly after that arm was raised in greeting? It didn't take long for Phyllis to push someone to the limit with her vicious tongue, I remembered. One comment was often enough. It must have been a spur of the moment impulse to give her a shove into the lake. Something any one of us might have done. But then, any one of us would have seen her being snapped up by a stealthily lurking crocodile and tried to help her. At the very least, screamed a warning and run about shouting for assistance.

It couldn't have been premeditated. Could it? I thought not. But *post*-meditated? Did the word exist?

Disturbed, I slipped the photographs away in the depths of my sock drawer. I left them there until I decided what to do with them.

*   *   *

A week later I had still come to no decision and India was drawing further away from me, becoming a burnished memory and a series of well-worn stories. An e-mail message accompanied by two paper-clip symbols popped up onto my screen late one night. Inspector Hari Singh of the Rajasthan Police sent his compliments to Miss Hardwick and drew her attention to the following attachment.

'Affair officially of no further interest to the Indian Police. Action by architect, perhaps?' he had added mysteriously.

I got the first surprising enclosure up on screen. The inspector, I guessed, must have kept, all these weeks, an IT marker out on names he was interested in. I wondered briefly if my own had been on his list. I bet it had! And here, finally, was evidence that two names had sprung his electronic trap. It was a page from the 'Daily Telegraph' of London, two days ago. The Court and Social page. Bemused but intrigued, I had read down to the end of the 'Forthcoming Marriages' column before I saw it. 'Professor Timothy Wickham-Skeith of

150

Oxford and Ms. Paula Parrish of Godalming. The engagement is announced between . . .'

I summoned up the second attachment. Another print-out from an English paper. Yesterday's 'Oxford Post'. The same information was on offer but with the accompaniment of a colour photograph of the happy pair. Tim was looking much younger, fit and tanned, I thought. Paula was looking up at him with glowing eyes. She had changed her green silk shirt for a vibrant pink one, to echo her romantic mood perhaps. The article 'Love amongst the ruins' told how the bereaved professor had found consolation. Love had apparently blossomed under a fragrant frangipani tree in the ruins of the royal city of Fatepur Sikhri. Did this sound like the first beat on the drum of publicity? To my suspicious mind it did.

I remembered the determined figure on the lake path and thoughtfully took out the triptych of photographs. 'Poor old Timothy! Poor old feller!' I thought. 'Out of the frying pan . . .' And I knew what the inspector was urging me to do.

I hit the reply button and sent back a short message: 'Action taken this day.' Then I found an envelope and slipped the three photographs inside. I added a note of the 'thought this might be of some interest' type, signed it, copied the professor's address from the screen onto the envelope and stuck a first-class stamp on it.

He'd work it out. If he wanted to.

RUTH McGAVIN

Ruth (Bonsall) McGavin was brought up in a very unusual environment! Along with her love of music, literature and a special interest in people, she has travelled widely.

A hospital training was put to good use in Central Asia, where Ruth and her husband Murray, an eye surgeon, lived and worked for several years. They have three children – David, Andrew and Carrie – one of whom has played professional rugby (not Carrie!), following in the footsteps of Murray, a Scottish rugby trialist.

A Scottish MA degree from Glasgow University later led to a post for Ruth at Bedford School, where she was asked to set up an EFL Department, for teaching English to foreign students.

Murray continues to work in the prevention of world blindness, and together they are now setting up a Christian Trust, seeking to alleviate suffering and promote health and education in developing countries.